The Director

and Other Stories from Morocco

Modern Middle East
Literatures in Translation Series

The Director
and Other Stories from Morocco

Leila Abouzeid

Introduction by
Elizabeth Warnock Fernea

The Center for Middle Eastern Studies
The University of Texas at Austin

Library of Congress Catalogue Card Number: 2005931342
ISBN: 0-292-71265-0

Printed in the United States of America

Cover photograph by Ronald Baker
Cover design by Diane Watts
Series Editor: Annes McCann-Baker

The Center gratefully acknowledges financial support for the publication of *The Director and Other Stories from Morocco* from the National Endowment for the Arts in Washington, D.C.

Table of Contents

Author's Preface

Like most novelists, east and west, I began my literary career in 1978 with a short story that I thought was the first step toward writing a novel. When I wrote *Year of the Elephant*, I included in the volume the eight stories I had produced while patiently waiting for that novel to come to fruition in my imagination. The stories were too few to be published separately, and I had decided I would write no more in the genre after that.

Critics and students focused on the novel *Year of the Elephant* and seemed to ignore the stories. Even I paid no attention to the fact that no study had appeared on them in Arabic. I knew only too well that the short story is not held in high esteem in Morocco. The genre is receding as an art form before the fact of the novel all over the Arab world. We in the Middle East and the Maghreb have no short-story critical theory, studies, or symposiums. Arab publishers back away from the short story. Arab readers believe it is easy because it is short, and they assume that they are supposed to read it in a newspaper or listen to it on the radio, because they think it to be part of the business of entertainment rather than that of scholarship. Except for the Egyptian Yusuf Idris, an Arab writer mainly of short stories is yet to be born.

I have, I must admit, shared this general view, until critic John Maier from the State University of New York at Brockport wrote a couple of thought-provoking pieces on two of the eight stories in *Year of the Elephant*.[1] Copies of these works came to me, by chance, as a translator was working on a French version of *Year of the Elephant* and simply decided that he was going to exclude the stories "because a French publisher would not combine two literary genres." He added, however, "These stories can be published separately in France, if you would write some more." And that is how this new set evolved.

As I was working on the English version of the new stories, I realized that the translation had gone beyond my familiarity with my native tongue. It allowed me to pause and look at my stories through the lens of a foreign language with a magnified scope. I knew their cultural connotations and linguistic concepts. Thus could I prevent misunderstandings and false interpretations.

My literal translation, however, needed the literary enhancement of an editor, such as that of the talented Elizabeth Fernea, whose work on this set contributed the proficiency of a first-class writer.

I was pleasantly surprised that in spite of the current status of the short story, these stories were enthusiastically welcomed by two reputable publishers, the Lebanese Al-markaz atthaqafi al-arabi for the original version, and the Center for Middle Eastern Studies at the University of Texas at Austin for the English version.

I hope the stories will be appreciated by the readers as well and help remove that mindset that has been incumbent upon the short story so far.

Leila Abouzeid
Rabat, January 7, 2005

[1] John Maier, "Exchanging Strangeness: Fiction of Jane Bowles and Leila Abouzeid," in *Mirrors on the Maghrib: Critical Reflections on Paul and Jane Bowles and Other American Writers in Morocco*, ed. Kevin R. Lacey and Francis Poole (Delmar, NY: Caravan Books, 1996), 151-184; and "Leila Abouzeid's 'Divorce,'" in *Desert Songs, Western Images of Morocco and Moroccan Images of the West* (Albany: State University of New York Press, 1996).

Introduction

The maverick literary genre known as the short story has become increasingly popular in the West since its beginnings in the nineteenth century. But in other cultures the short story is a relatively new phenomenon. Leila Abouzeid, author of the stories presented here, herself states that "the short story" is not held in high esteem in Morocco, her own homeland. Further, the short story, she believes, "is receding ... before the fact of the novel" all over the Arab world.

In the West, critics and readers debate the definition of a short story. It may be called a truncated narrative, part of an unfinished novel, or a vignette, a brief snapshot of a character or an event. As Hortense Calisher wrote some years ago, "A short story is a tempest in a tea-cup." What some critics mean by a "truncated narrative" is a tale which begins in the middle. The reader assumes that some of the action has taken place before the story begins. The writer proceeds to continue that previous action and brings the tale to a conclusion, a conclusion in which something has changed in the lives of one or more of the characters.

The definitions—vignette, unfinished novel, or truncated narrative—have never, however, prevented writers in past centuries from experimenting with different forms to achieve their storytelling goal. In Western letters, for example, the stories of William Faulkner, Sarah Orne Jewett, Paul Bowles, Isaak Dinesen, and Jean Stafford vary enormously in theme, plot, context, setting, characters, and expository style.

So it is with writers in other cultures, as the short story begins to appear in Africa, the Middle East, Latin America, and Asia. Many of these older cultures have an advantage in attempting the short story: the much-admired storyteller, one who is in the so-called oral tradition. In the Middle East, the Arabian Nights stories remain an influence, but so do the tales of grandparents and professional storytellers.

Leila Abouzeid's new stories exhibit some of these influences, but as an artist she takes the story in new directions. "Grandfather's Story," for example, is indeed exactly what the title announces, but Abouzeid has set it in a new frame: it is "the only story my maternal grandfather ever told us" (11), and she questions all the assumptions about orally-communicated stories. Was Grandfather really illiterate (most traditional storytellers are so characterized)? If so, how did he learn the archaic Arabic terms with which his story is peppered? The reader begins to see the "oral tradition" in a new light.

Some of Abouzeid's stories follow what might be termed an expected short-story form, but "From the Diary of a Parliamentary Employee" is clearly of another, newer mold. Many of the stories are indeed truncated narratives, in the sense that the tale begins in the middle, and the reader is expected to assume that some of the action has taken place before the story begins. This is particularly effective when both the past and present of Morocco are concerned.

Abouzeid uses different styles and forms to approach the "new" Morocco. In "A Genius Filmmaker" and "The Director," she criticizes the "new" professionals who have learned from the West but, she suggests, have been corrupted in the process. She, the writer, is often the protagonist. Events in her own life—travel to Britain, encounters with French residents who have chosen to stay in Morocco at the end of the colonial rule—are the basis for subtle critiques of foreign customs and mores, as in "Mrs. O'Grady," "A Paying Guest," "Medi," "A Jealous Wife," and "Phone Call."

Problems of readjustment to a different world are also the subject matter for stories such as "What Attitude?" "The Trade Unionist," and "Her Best Friend." "The Bathing Suit" is a kind of reverie—a remembrance of an earlier time in Moroccan history and a comparison of past and present.

The story "Abderrahim" comes close to fulfilling Hortense Calisher's definition of a short story as "a tempest in a tea-cup." This sad tale of a young man whose talent for singing was seen as shameful by his traditional father does indeed demonstrate a potential for explosion. Abouzeid here becomes a commentator, entering the story to criticize the father's cruel action which leads to Abderrahim's death. "This young man was constantly on my mind," she writes. "I imagined the father really very old now, walking slowly, slowly. I imagined his loneliness in the large, cold, and empty house.... He could not have absorbed all that tragedy so naturally.... Deep inside, he must have regretted his actions and must now blame himself" (61). Abouzeid criticizes the story itself. "Were it my story, I would send the father to jail or at least make him sink in depression.... I would have [Abderrahim] reject the father's tyranny, and I would give the women some presence in the scene, the mother at any rate" (60).

Tragedy and pathos are present in the collection, as is irony—a stage in the acceptance of the new nation-state and attempts to deal with the states' new demands. "The Baker" is a triumphant conclusion—a boy who is expelled from the new government school becomes first a baker's apprentice and then a master baker who becomes so wealthy that he eventually supports his educated siblings and his parents in old age.

As Abouzeid utilizes different styles and forms to reflect different experiences and different emotional moods, the reader glimpses elements of everyday life for the men and women in the young nation-state of Morocco.

The work contradicts the author's own statement that the short story is "receding." This collection demonstrates a new vigor and variety in the form, in Morocco, at least.

Elizabeth Warnock Fernea

The Director

and Other Stories from Morocco

The Bathing Suit

"You were Snow White, weren't you?" said the young girl, turning the pages of an album and patting the photos underneath their plastic sheet.

"I used to weigh forty-five kilos," said the mother proudly.

"Tight dresses too, above the knee, and matching shoes and bags."

"They said: 'Take off the veil!' and we did what we were told."

"Who said?"

"The King and the scholars. It felt like taking off one's skin. They said: 'A woman's virtue is her veil. That piece of material has only isolated women, loaded them with helplessness, ignorance, and manipulation. It has bestowed on them underdevelopment and submissiveness.' As the poet says: 'Don't you see that they've grown servile because they grew up in the laps of bondmaids?'

"So we took the veil off."

"And now, they're telling us to wear it again."

"Because the first unveiling turned to nudity, and liberty became libertinism."

"Women, women, women! Yesterday, today, and forever."

"They're the heart of the matter, because they're catalysts for change and the guardians of tradition."

The young girl stared at the photos and said: "Is this really you?"

"No, it's not. Forty years stand between her and me."

"You wore mini-skirts?"

"And shorts. They were part of a bathing suit, as a matter of fact."

"I didn't know you swam."

"I have never swum in my whole life."

"Is this an enigma, a riddle, a joke, or what exactly?"

"No. I simply wore a bathing suit for my sports classes, under a T-shirt. It was a dark blue one, with white streaks, large stripes, and a back down to the waist. I can still see the run in its right leg, as I see that stain on your white shirt."

"My stain is the fault of your saffron dishes! But I won't remember it forty years from now."

Vivid memories came to the mother's mind of her own childhood. She said in a low voice:

"My father lived in another town with a woman. One day at the beginning of summer holidays, he dropped by, saying that he was going to take us on vacation and I was to accompany him to his work place in his town to see for myself, well aware no one was believing him. But when I came back, my sister did not listen and my mother looked away in contempt. My mother said, 'When I gave him my gold bracelets, I thought a nice show or movie in this life of ours between walls is better than bracelets lying in a wardrobe. I said this to him, so he would behave himself. I told him to sell them and get us a TV set. I didn't want him to say that I had brought a TV set into the house without his permission. Then we waited and waited and didn't see that TV set until after a whole year.'

"'Yes, yes of course,' I said, 'but I did see him sign and I did hear him say: *Mister administrator, you say that you give priority to people who have kids. Here's my kid, so you know who I want that cabin for.*'

"'I know who he wants it for,' my mother retorted with a contemptuous, twisted mouth. I glanced at my sister, and she gave me a look as much as to say: 'She's right.'

"'He convinced you, didn't he?' my mother said to me.

"'It's you who are overly suspicious,' I replied. 'By God, what will it cost you to give him one more chance?' She shot a direct look at me and I insisted. 'One little last chance.'

"'Shut up!' my mother burst out, raising her finger at me. 'I know him. He's careless, yes! He gave you nothing but talk and you'll be sorry, I'm telling you. You vouched for him. Didn't you?'

"'Don't anticipate. Please,' I said.

"'I long for the sea,' broke in the sister, as if thinking aloud.

"'Splashing and castle building, huh?' I incited her.

"'Running before a wild wave, then stopping, bending with my hands on my knees, laughing fierce laughter,' she returned in a stately tone, straightening her back as if she was delivering a speech.

"And I added: 'Picking up floating, tender seaweed in the water through flickers of light.'

"'Dipping my feet in soft, damp sand where worn waves deposit their bubbles, as birds hover over a quiet sea, their whiteness turned pink in the twilight.'

"'Enough!' said my mother, spreading and gathering the edge of her long robe. 'Stop it.'

"'It's you who're overly suspicious,' I repeated and then resorted to the Qur'an for an effective persuasion: 'Indeed some suspicion is a sin.'[1]

"And she softened, because she said: 'I do trust God.'

"I cannot say that she was convinced but she gave in. So plans began with the following list."

> Bathing suit (2).
> Beach towel (2).
> Hat (2).

The young girl leafed through the album saying: "I cannot see any pictures of that. And you're talking of two sets of each item, as if Grandma were not there."

"She was there all right, but she had to make do with watching, because that kind of liberation was not for her generation," the mother answered, gesturing backwards with her thumb before pointing to the rest of the list.

> Tan cream (2).
> Sun glasses (2).
> Bathing cap (2).

The mother continued about her own mother, "But your grandmother said that there was no need for the cream, because she was going to make a blend of boiled henna leaves and olive oil for us, which would give a much better tan, and that we should limit the list to what's absolutely necessary. So we also dropped the hat, the sunglasses and the bathing cap.

"Finally, my sister chose a red bathing suit and a towel in the same color, with a white sail on it, and I, a dark blue bathing suit and a towel in the same color full of wavy lines, starfish, spiral shells, and a big black sun surrounded with a kind of pointed teeth."

"You remember all these details?"

"I do, as if I were looking at them now."

"And then you went back home in euphoria of course."

"Oh, I forgot. We also bought that novel by Yusuf Essubai, called *I Am Departing*. It was all the rage then, causing readers to shed buckets of tears. I said to my sister: 'I'll read it while sitting on a rock full of holes, in front of shallow pools of clear water. Do you know the pleasure of reading in a place like that? You don't, of course.' But my sister said she was going to rest and relax, not to read and cry."

The mother said, "My mother tucked up her skirts, rolled up her sleeves, wrapped her apron around her, and began stirring eggs as she sat on the floor. She combined the baking powder with the dough. 'This baking powder is from the year before the last,' she explained proudly, and then quoted a popular saying: 'Save things, not men, for the former will one day be of use but the latter one day will stun you.'

"I exchanged a glance with my sister, then turned to my mother: 'Are you convinced now?' 'Yes and no,' Mother said, combining the other items and rolling the mixture into balls that she placed on a greased pan. She shoved the pan into the oven and tackled the cabinets. She took out spices, flour, dried vegetables, salt, sugar, tea, coffee, oil, even washing powder, fine wire sponges, black soap, laundry clips, the floor rug, and the broom. She put all these things in plastic bags fastened with brown adhesive tape she had brought back earlier from the market. She had also brought plastic sandals she said she was going to wear for late afternoon walks, when there were fewer people on the beach.

"'Next, you're going to take along the roof duster,' said my sister. 'Remember, you're going to Mohamadia beach, not to the Arabian desert.' But my mother said she'd take the pressure cooker as well. 'The administrator,' I put in, 'said that the cabin we've rented is fully equipped and you can buy everything in Mohamadia.'

"She neatly stacked the plastic bags. 'Oh no,' she said clapping her mouth. 'We forgot the suitcase. I've got to go to the medina now. That paper suitcase of mine has grown flabby and peeled; its latches are broken. And the parasol! You wouldn't want us to use blankets as sun shade like some country bumpkins, would you?'

4

"And so saying, she removed the cookies from the oven, but they were one flat disc cemented to the pan. She made another set only to come up with the same result. She sat bewildered. 'Keep things, not men, hmmm?' I said, lifting up the empty baking powder packages from the year before the last. She pushed the pan away, disregarding the whole thing, put on her *djellabah*, and said: 'I'm gonna drop by the medina now.'

"As soon as she came back, she began to recite what had happened: 'How much is that suitcase, Mustapha?' I asked. 'Two hundred,' he replied. And she went on relating what she said and what he said and how she finally succeeded in dropping the price in half. When she went to bed, she was still smiling. I lay down but could not sleep.

"The next morning I woke up with the birds, went to the bathroom, and turned on the tap. It rushed in an uproar, but Mother turned over and resumed her snoring. My sister looked at me absently and said: 'Have you put the plane in the garage?' and fell back into sleep.

"I opened a book but could not see anything but the forms of the letters. I went to the kitchen and put on the coffee. I thought they would not be able to resist the odor. Then I turned the radio on. The voice of Hussein El Bacha came out in its refreshing morning flavor: 'Bring your head down and breathe out. Bring your head up and breathe in.' I went to the balcony door, opened it, and folded the panels back in a clamor. The glass doors flashed in the rising sun. 'Heavens!' my mother interjected in a sleepy voice, screwing up her eyes to shut away the brightness. 'Come on! Wake up, you couple of sleepyheads! The sun is all over the place. We don't have time to waste.'

"I checked the suitcase, and said out loud: 'My bathing suit is there all right.' 'Smart girl,' my mother yawned mockingly. I took the suitcase in both hands. I wrestled the boxes, carried the parasol still in its plastic bag, and put everything within reach by the front door. My sister came out of the bathroom, smoothing her hair, and singing Abdelhalim's song: "Drive In the Parasols!" She paused to exclaim: '*On va partir en vacances! Ça va être génial!*' Then, resorting to Arabic, she shouted out in an angry tone: 'What am I supposed to do now?' 'You can detach those cookies.' 'I need an axe, tsk, tsk.' She went on her way, with that chuckle of hers which sounded like a soft wave splash.

"At the appointed time we were all dressed and sitting by the baggage like travelers in a station platform, waiting for our father to come. Half an hour passed, and my mother blew agitatedly until the hem of her face veil trembled. 'Moroccan eight o'clock is nine, as a matter of fact,' I said soothingly, but she began complaining: 'It's an old practice of his. Like when he forgot me in a hotel room. We were on our way to his hometown after our wedding. We had stopped on the way to spend a night in a hotel. He said he was gonna buy some food. Then he locked the door from the outside and disappeared. I didn't see him until the next day, and I was a bride. He said he had forgotten me.'

"'There you go back to your old doubts again!' I said, striding to the balcony. I bent over, looked up and down the street, then returned, lowering my head. Somebody rattled the front door handle. My sister flung it open. 'The electricity company clerk,' she said in a flat voice, making way for the man.

"When the second half hour struck, I got up to my feet and started taking off my outdoor clothes. My sister did the same thing. Mother stripped off her djellabah and we took all the baggage out of the way."

The young girl sat still, her elbows planted on the old photo album, her chin resting on her clasped hands, her wide eyes opened wider.

"It was there and then that we decided to shake off our fear," the mother went on about her childhood. "We put our bathing suits on underneath our dresses, took the towels, the parasol, and the lunch, and jumped into a taxi bound for a nearby village with a well-known beach. But at the village, we found out that the beach was at least five kilometers away. So we walked down a winding road amid fields of high dried stalks and wilted yellow wild flowers; the indigo blue of the ocean spread down below us, way back to where it seemed to touch the arch of the sky. 'Oh my!' exclaimed my sister. 'God has certainly made his creation beautiful,' my mother exclaimed. 'What a good idea it was to come here,' I retorted. 'If this is just the Atlantic,' my sister added, 'how is the Mediterranean?'

"Soon we found ourselves face to face with a deserted shore, rimmed with rocks. It was after three p.m. 'God Almighty!' my mother exclaimed. We found we had taken the wrong road. So we decided to eat.

"We ate as waves broke against those rocks. Then we proceeded along the shore looking for the beach. When we finally arrived, the sun was setting. Anxiety came upon my mother, and she decided to go right back to the village, so that darkness would not catch us in this wasteland, as she put it. We all went back, having gained nothing but sore feet."

"She took you to the sea and brought you back dry, as the saying goes," the young girl said with a forced laugh, the photo album still open on her knees.

"We joked about my mother's anxiety," her mother went on, "and we said to her: 'You're always like that, scared of your own shadow.' But when we arrived at the village and found its square empty, no one around except for a few figures entering the little mosque and no taxis in sight, my mother began saying: 'What shall we do, God?' We caught her fear. And what do you think we did?"

"What?" the young girl inquired earnestly.

"We went to the railway station. But only one train stopped there, and it was at midnight. It was a small village with just one street lined with a grocery store, a butcher, a café, and a grill. Low street lights flickered through eucalyptus leaves. The street ended in a lonely area, like a scary one I had once seen in a dream.

"The station was empty except for two clerks and a hissing kerosene stove with their dinner cooking on it. The first was an old man in a worn uniform and hat, the second a well-built young man in regular clothes, with frizzed dark hair and a muddy complexion. They knew from our appearance what brought us to the village and our dilemma. 'You shouldn't have taken these kids through this kind of adventure,' the young man scolded my mother. 'We were bored, sir,' my mother answered in an ingratiating and complaining tone.

"I didn't like him interfering like that and I didn't like mother's tone. Later, he poured the contents of the cooking pot into a white enamel dish, a meat and turnip stew in too much water. He began breaking the bread and inviting us to eat, but we stepped back and firmly declined. I can still see that scene in my mind.

"So anyway, we finally got home, and I felt like a drowned person who's been rescued. We were exhausted, frightened, hungry, and sleepy. 'What a day!' my mother exclaimed. 'May he carry that experience on his shoulders on the day of judgment.' 'Who? Father?' I asked. 'Who else?'"

"What did Grandma mean?" the young girl inquired, shutting the old photo album.

"She was referring to the august utterance of the prophet: 'Verily, any one of you who takes anything unrightfully will meet God on the Day of Judgment carrying it. And I will know for sure which of you is meeting God carrying a camel lowing or a cow mooing or a sheep bleating.'[2] Mother meant that the ordeal we had been through that day was Father's fault."

"Nowadays," the young girl said, "people get condos illegally, and cars, villas, hotels, and apartment buildings. Imagine someone coming to meet God on the Day of Judgment with a car on his shoulders or a villa or an apartment building. Imagine!"

"God save us from that!" returned her mother. "So anyway, we had spent all our money and didn't know what to do with those bathing suits, towels, the parasol, plastic sandals, and suitcase."

"You could have preserved them," the young girl put in, jokingly. "They could be of use, as Grandma would've said."

"They were indeed, except for the parasol and the suitcase. My mother slipped them under the bed. I never knew what became of them. As for the sandals, she began wearing them to wash the apartment, on laundry day, and in the bathhouse. The beach towels were transformed into bath towels. When they wore out we cut them into kitchen rugs. My own bathing suit became shorts. I've never talked of it before, and I never thought it was still so present with me. Now I realize that I hated it!"

"You shouldn't have kept it, the memory of it in all these pictures."

"But that's what happened," returned the mother briskly.

---

[1] Qur'an. Al- Hujurat (The Apartments). Verse 12.
[2] Saheeh Al-Bukhary. Volume IV. Chapter 15 (Worker's fraud in getting a donation).

Grandfather's Story

This is the only story my maternal grandfather ever told us, because men, in our society, usually do not tell stories. That kind of thing is associated with women and with professional storytellers who frequent public squares, begging for money in exchange for their tales. That is undoubtedly why writers in my country took a long time to start writing novels. And even when they finally did, they were careful to call themselves novelists rather than that degrading title of "storyteller."

So I can recall only one story of Grandfather's, first as I said, because it was unusual for him to tell stories and also because the story was one that one remembers, including its content, characters, narration, language, dialogue, monologue, scenery, imagery, and atmospheres. (Of course, I only thought this later.)

I am not saying that Grandmother's stories were of lower quality. Not at all. Hers were set in her town. They were about women in their homes, men in their fields and shops, people and places we know, and events from here and now. Grandmother's stories were about betrayal and illicit love and were told in an ancient vernacular that has disappeared now with the opening of the gates of the old cities and the coming of radio and television.

Grandfather's story, on the other hand, is set in a faraway land and a remote time. It has anonymous characters and focuses on poverty and wealth, this life and the hereafter, the day of reckoning, and the balance of sins and good deeds, and all is told in an old manner of speech.

When I think of him, I see him pointing his hand and saying furiously: "You're misquoting," using a difficult word, I later discovered, derived from classical Arabic. I see him in a faded yellow wool djellabah and a white turban. I never saw him without the turban, which he wrapped around his head twenty times, and which, when it was not wrapped, stretched from the inner room to the outside courtyard.

He resembled Hemingway with his short white beard, fine-featured face, large shoulders, and well-built body. If you put a djellabah and a turban on Hemingway, he would have looked like my grandfather.

He would say: "I'm cold," or "I'm hungry," or "I'm happy from head to toe," using an archaic way of speech. Then he would ask: "Do you understand? You don't, of course." He would explain and add: "You just throw words around without understanding the weight of a mustard seed in them. Mustard is African rue." And then he would intone: "And we shall set balances for the Day of Judgment. Then, no one will be wronged at all, even if it be by the weight of a grain of a mustard seed."[1]

For a long time, I thought that mustard was African rue. It was the only mistake Grandfather made, at least the only one I came across, and one for which I have never forgiven him. Then he would come out with a string of strange words and point out their origin in classical Arabic, reciting from the Qur'an and quoting a statement of the third Caliph Uthman, adding: "You hear words in your vernacular you think have come from the middle of nowhere, and they are Arabic!"

I smile at the memory, as I write this, because a story has popped into my head: A Moroccan man in Paris went out looking for shoe-strings and asking for *les sirs*, thinking that the Arabic *seer* came from French. Arabs did not have shoes, of course, but they had sandals, and their "seer" was the leather string they placed between their toes. That is where the modern connotation of the word comes from, as *qitar* (train) comes from the qitar of a string of camels in the straight line of a caravan. Here, I am scratching words up like Grandfather.

Was Grandfather educated? If he was, why can I not recall a single image of him reading or writing? And why did I never see in his house a book or a pen or even a small notebook? There were carved shelves painted dark green, but they held only big antique bowls decorated with crescents and stars in faded green and brown. There were never books. And if he had been able to read, there would have been a copy of the Qur'an, at least.

But if he was illiterate, how did he know about the classical Arabic origins of all those strange words? And Uthman's statement? Or did he simply pick it all up at the mosque? Yes, he was wrong about the mustard seed, but he was right on all the other matters.

I also do not know where he got this single story of his, nor the circumstances that made him give up his seriousness and sit in our midst to tell fairy tales. When he told the story, there was a grandeur about him, elegance, and good looks, and he was, unusually for him, in a good mood, speaking in an articulate, delicate voice:

"Once upon a time (but God, the most wise, most powerful and most generous, knows about the unseen in his realms), there was a fisherman who lived in the land of the Turkomen. He was very tall and had a large head, but he was a poor man with a wife and children.

"One day he went to the sea, said *bismillahi arrahmani rraheem* (in the name of God, the most merciful, the most compassionate), cast his net, and waited, but when he pulled it out, there was nothing in it but seaweed. 'There is no power or strength except in God,' he said. 'What kind of a damn day is this?' he added, but immediately regretted his swearing. He cleaned the net and cast it again to no avail. He stayed like that for three days, pulling the empty net out, spreading it to dry, and going back home full of a sadness so great that only God could know its amount.

"On the fourth day when the imam of the mosque came for the dawn prayer, he found the fisherman sleeping at the foot of a pillar, with his head on his net. The imam waited until the prayer was over, then went to him and said: 'Servant of God, why do I see you sad and subjugated? And what made you sleep in the mosque? Tell me so I can hear it from you.'

"'I'm at my wits' end sir. I've lost interest in time and space, for the sea grew hostile to me. For the last three days, it has given me nothing but weeds. And because my children are hungry, I feared to return home.'

"And he had a good cry. When the imam heard that, he said to him: 'Let's go to that sea, brother.' 'I hear and obey,' replied the fisherman. He shouldered his net and picked up his slippers, and the two of them made their way down to the sea. The minute they arrived, the imam raised a call indicating the imminent beginning of prayer. He performed two long, splendid bowings and prostrations, reciting verses of the Qur'an in a psalmody so charming that if they had heard it, birds would have stood still in the air and sheep would have stopped grazing.

"When he finished, he raised his palms and made the following supplication: 'God! Thee who said to Mohamed, and your saying is truth, that when your servants asked, to say you were close and would answer the call of the caller.[2] You who provide for birds in the sky and for fish in the water, provide for your servant. If his livelihood is difficult, make it easy. If it's far, make it near. If it's meager, make it plenty, for his hardship has been long, his misfortune severe. His children's eyes have sunk, their faces have paled, their bodies have wilted, and their moans have risen. Lord, Thy servant's livelihood is in the sea, bring it out as Thee brought out Yunus from the whale's belly, as Thee told Abraham's fire not to burn and Ishmael's knife not to cut. There's no power and no strength except in Thee. There is no God but Thee. I ask Thy forgiveness and penitence. And God's prayer and peace be upon our lord Mohamed, his family, companions, and followers till the Day of Judgment.'

"As the iman was pronouncing that prayer, the fisherman raised his hands, bowed his head, and said: 'Amen!'

"Finally, the imam said to him: 'Come on, brother, cast your net now with the benediction of God.'

"Much obliged, the fisherman kissed the imam's hand and went into the sea.

"By midday he was on his way to town with a good load of mullet. He was very happy, and he said to himself: 'All the credit for this goes to God. It'll be, *inshallah*, a good bargain.'

"By the afternoon prayer time, he had made a profit on the sale. He went to the baker and bought round loaves of white bread. Then he went to the food seller and bought mutton and headed happily home.

Before he reached his house, he saw an orphan and the poor woman who accompanied him at their usual spot in their filthy tatters.

"'Cleanliness also needs money,' he thought to himself. 'These two now are hungrier than me and my kids, and God praises those who prefer others above themselves even though there is want among them.[3] He also says, and His saying is truth, that you cannot attain virtue unless you spend of what you love.[4] And I do love white bread and mutton.' And so saying, he put the bread and mutton in front of the woman. The child gave him a smile that went straight to his heart and filled it with joy.

"Thereupon God opened the gates of profit to him. The fisherman started going every day to the market with the best kind of fish and selling it for a good price. Before long, he was one of the wealthiest people in town and took to distributing white bread and mutton to the poor each and every Friday.

"One night he saw in a dream the Day of Judgment and two angels talking about him. One said to the other: 'These are the balances of the Day of Judgment and these are his deeds.'

"But the list of his sins was long. The angel said: 'Is there anything left?' 'There's his Friday feeding of the poor,' the other answered. His Friday alms were put in the scale, but they didn't outweigh his sins. 'Is there anything left?' the angel again asked. 'There's the child's smile.' The smile was put in the scale of good deeds and dropped it down to the ground with its weight."

Grandfather stopped. His glance wandered expressively over us. His eyes were half closed like a rooster's. We sat there, mesmerized.

---

[1] Qur'an. (The Prophets). Verse 47.

[2] Qur'an. (The Cow). Verse 186.

[3] Qur'an. (The Gathering). Verse 9.

[4] Qur'an. (The Family of 'Imran). Verse 92.

A Jealous Wife

I was introduced to Bahija by her husband, which in our society is quite unusual. I had bought him books abroad, and he invited me to dinner in her name, in the European manner. A married couple, colleagues of theirs on his newspaper, were there as well. During dinner, the host talked about his latest story, one about Moroccan immigrants in Europe. He said that some Moroccan women in Holland are completely cut off in their homes and speak nothing but their Berber dialect.

"Did you meet them?" asked his colleague "Did you talk to them?"

"Talk to them? How could I? Don't you know how the uprising started in the Reef Mountains?[1] I didn't want to get in trouble with their husbands."

"It's hard to imagine the life of those women," said the colleague. "You don't see that kind of estrangement anywhere else in the world."

"Well, you don't think you know everything in the world, do you?" snorted the colleague's wife. They both tried to speak at once, but she stood up to him. "We were in Djeddah once," she went on, now that she had silenced her husband and had the floor all to herself. "My mother, two old women, myself, and a lot of luggage. You can imagine the luggage of four women coming back from pilgrimage.

"We rented a pick-up and told the driver to take us to a hotel. But he said we needed police permission to go to a hotel, because we were not escorted by a man. So, the pick-up driver took us to the police station where we were received by a large cop, fairly bulging out of his khaki uniform. His eyelids were darkened with *kohl* powder and his palms dyed red with henna."

"He must have been a new bridegroom," said the host. "I met a Sudanese couple in Geneva once. They both had their palms dyed with henna, and it was obvious that they were newlyweds. That Saudi policeman must have been in the same situation."

"I don't know," said the narrator. "What's more curious is that *every* time we tried to argue with him, he repeated: 'Non-escorted women are not allowed in hotels.' 'And where shall we sleep?' cried out one of the old women. 'In the street?' 'It's the law!' cried back the policeman."

"Does the law there anticipate cases like this?" asked the host.

"I don't know, but he did mention the law. Outside," continued our narrator, "I made for the pick-up and asked the driver to be patient. The old women were dismayed. A worn, old Egyptian woman, wearing a head veil and a European dress, stopped to ask why they were upset, then offered to take them home. When I joined them, she asked, alarmed, pointing at me: 'Is she with you? Then, no! Come on Mohamed,' she said, dragging a dark Saudi man in European trousers and a T-shirt with her, and they hurried away."

"She was pious enough," remarked the narrator's husband, "to take three old women into her marital home, but not a young one."

"The old women were more and more upset. The driver got out of the pick-up, wearing his loin cloth with its square print, his Gulf scarf tied around his head, his body so thin that you could not guess his age. He slammed the door of the truck, snatched a small stick to chew, and yelled at us: 'Well, ladies where to now?' Then he excused himself and stood there, pulling at his wisp of beard. The old woman who stood up to the policeman asked me in a lamenting tone: 'What'll become of us?'

"'We'll die martyrs,' I answered, teasing her, trying to relieve her anxiety.

"'But what're we going to do?' she insisted.

"'Let's go there!' I said seriously, pointing at a Saudi Airlines agency, across the road. 'We'll go there and ask for the Moroccan Embassy phone number.'"

"How clever!" snorted the narrator's husband stiffly.

"At that agency," she went on, ignoring him, "they said that they couldn't help us. They either didn't know the number or were busy. They did have a crowd. By this time, the old women were sobbing."

"Enough!" yelled the narrator's husband. He loosened his tie, lifted his chin, pursed his lips, and shook his head. "I have heard this story twenty times and I don't want to hear it again." The narrator came to a stand still, and her mouth fell open on her even teeth. Bahija, startled, froze. Her husband emitted something like a laugh and turned to me: "This is marriage! Good for you who stayed single."

18

"Good I stayed single," I echoed mechanically, not knowing where to look. The narrator took a sip of water and went on arrogantly, her fingers clasping the glass.

"The old women's anxiety was contagious and I tried to overcome it. At that point, I heard someone asking me, 'What's up?' It was a bareheaded, plump man with a shaved face, in a tight Saudi robe. 'This is my mother,' I explained 'and two old ladies we met at Mecca. I'm somewhat responsible for them. Our plane leaves tomorrow, and we are not allowed to stay in hotels.'

"'I'm Tunisian,' he said. 'I work in a bank here and I live in a hotel. Come with me. I'll say that you're my relatives.'"

"Did you go with him?" inquired the host. "Did you trust him?"

"We had no choice. His name was Nurdeen Lemrabet. See how I can still remember it? As if it were a story. If it were a story and he were to read it, he would recognize himself. He led the way inside the old part of Djeddah, striding, catching his robe up, and clacking his sandals along the streets. We followed him. I was behind, with my mother leaning on me. I did grow anxious when our marching in those old streets went on and on. But that Tunisian was like this!" She split the air with the edge of her hand to demonstrate the man's straight carriage.

"What about the pick-up?" I asked to relax the atmosphere.

"It trailed behind like a snail."

"How much did the driver charge you after that marathon?" asked the host.

"I don't know. It was the Tunisian gentleman who paid him. Besides, all he wanted by then, I guess, was to get rid of us." She stopped for us to laugh, but we did not.

"Is that it?" asked her husband. "Not interesting."

"I didn't tell it as I would have liked to. You didn't help," she replied, looking away from him.

At that moment Bahija spoke for the first time, asking us to move to the next room to have tea. The host showed his colleague his article on Moroccan immigrants in Europe. "I've read it," said the latter, taking the paper and handing it over to his wife. She passed it to me, but the host recovered it and put it on a cupboard. "I want to look at it,"

I said politely, but he pushed it away with his finger tips by way of an answer.

"The newspapers will be after us," said the colleague, trying to make up for his gesture and insinuating something. We grinned at the joke: our host is nicknamed "paper man," because he always goes about with a package of newspapers under his arm. At that point, the journalist couple stood up to leave and I did the same thing.

Bahija's silence that evening disconcerted me. She either was shy, I thought, or upset by that fight between the married couple. But how could a journalist be shy, I wondered. I thought the second explanation was probably right. When I returned her invitation to dinner, two weeks later, she again said not a word. I did not want to jump, as a woman, to the obvious conclusion and say: "She's jealous." When I met the journalist's wife who had told the story at the dinner party, however, I asked her: "Have you seen Bahija recently?"

"Don't talk to me about her," she burst out. "I haven't seen her since that evening we were together. She doesn't trust women, you know."

"Maybe she doesn't trust her husband and has her reasons," I commented. "So she's jealous, huh?"

"Like a cat. Frankly, I couldn't believe it when I saw that she had invited you that evening."

After I realized the reason of Bahija's annoyance, I severed all my connections with her and her husband. As for her, she changed directions whenever she saw me in the street. Eventually, she slipped out of my mind completely.

One morning when I was in a taxi stopped at a traffic light, I saw her husband crossing the street with his package of newspapers. He was leaning on a beautiful stick. Had it not been for the papers, I would not have recognized him. He was bent, his hair had fallen out, and he was so skinny that his trousers flapped as if nobody were wearing them. I decided that he had been struck by cancer.

A few days later, I met Bahija in the crowd at the vegetable market. Actually, she saw me and called and waved, plowing ahead through the crowd.

"I haven't seen you for ages," she said as soon as she came to me. "Where have you been?"

"Here, and you?"

"In London. I have been working there for the last three years." As she proudly mentioned the name of the paper, the image of her husband, crossing the street with his skinny body, flashed through my mind. "I do come back to Rabat on holidays," she explained. "I still have my apartment. I won't give it up. The rent is cheap, from an older time, and my husband lives there anyway. An Arab newspaper wanted to hire him, but when they found out he was sick, they hired me instead."

She turned to leave but looked back and said: "Stay in touch with him, will you? He's so lonely." She rummaged in her bag for a note book, wrote down her husband's phone number, and handed it over to me. "Do call him. Have a cup of coffee with him," she insisted and disappeared in the crowd. I stood there with my hand over my mouth until I heard some one yell: "Get out of the way!"

---

[1] The uprising in the Reef Mountains started in 1957, because the mayor's men in that northern area of Morocco ordered women to remove their face veils when writing down their characteristics on their ID cards.

The Director

It was the first visit ever, for their relationship had slackened somewhat since the aunt had married and moved to the capital. Administrative posting does wrench people away from their hometowns and tear their family ties asunder.

The visitor looked puzzled, and the aunt was seized by an increasing anxiety.

"Where've you been?" she finely said, fidgeting with the collar of her faded housedress. "None of you visits me."

"We would, if it wasn't for the long distance and work."

"There's no end to work in this world, is there? But what's this visit about, niece?"

"I've been transferred here, Aunt. And ever since I settled down, I've been thinking of visiting you. But I haven't had time."

"No blessing in time any more, eh, nor in anything else. How are you all?"

"Fine."

"I haven't seen you since…?" She counted on her fingers, as she stood up and walked out of the room, her plastic slippers clacking on the concrete floor.

Across the courtyard, the wall opposite had experienced humidity, its lower part mossy. Ragged shadows swing on it in the light of the setting sun and autumn breeze.

The house contained two rooms, one leading to the other. The inner one, probably the bedroom, was windowless. A full-length curtain, dropped on obscurity, assumed the function of a door. The furniture in the first room consisted of hard mattresses on banquettes of worn wood, upholstered in a cheap old fabric. A Turkish rug, mostly threadbare, covered the floor under a low table. On the middle wall, a wooden shelf held an accordion. In the corner sat a radio in the fifties style, on it a gold clock with pillars and a pendulum holding a ball inside a glass dome. The kind of clock the notables used to bring back from Tangier when you still needed a passport to go there.

Next to the watch was a picture of the husband on his big motorcycle, wearing boots and riding trousers, a tweed jacket, a cap molding his head with the earflaps turned down, enormous spectacles pushed up on his forehead, the kind used by pilots at the beginning of the century. He looks defiantly at the camera. The aunt is riding behind him with her face veil.

The photograph brought back to the visitor's mind that scene live, from when she was a girl of seven, and the couple had come back home for the first time, on that motorcycle. They had proceeded into town on foot, grinning. Children crowded and followed them. Women peeped out from roofs and doorways. Pedestrians stopped, and shopkeepers interrupted deals and stepped out of their stores.

The husband went on pushing the motorcycle in the alleys right to his in-laws' courtyard where it stood, sparkling in its metallic attire. The niece had walked around it without touching it, lest some device would burst or the whole thing would start off.

The aunt had been matched with the motorcycle in the little girl's mind, embodying for her modernity and prestige. As a matter of fact, the aunt had been the first woman in town to enter school under colonialism and had spent two years in it. That was why she knew a little French. As for Arabic, she stayed illiterate in it, not knowing the difference between a stick and an alif, the first letter in the alphabet.

Yet the aunt thinks of herself, right up to these days, as an educated, modern, enlightened, and unique woman, etc.... She wears her hair short and puts on sunglasses and European dresses made of satin with gold squares and voluminous, bell-shaped skirts. She reads, even though with difficulty, the *romans photos*, those love stories in the form of pictures, with lines of dialogue joined to the characters' mouths. She takes photographs, attends resorts and movie theaters, and carries her own identification card and passport.

What had made her leave school so soon? Marriage perhaps. For she had married a civil servant, "a great director" as she calls him, whose education level was hardly above hers. In those days, civil servants had been kinds of aristocrats in the public eye, combining as they did education (even if it was of a low level), enlightenment, prestige, and money. When she moved to the capital with him, her own prestige went up and she became a model of fashion, elegance, and modernity for the women of the town.

Her conversations were about herself and her things. "I bought," "I traveled," "I have," "My hairdresser," "My dress," "My seamstress."

"From the heart of Paris you know, the seamstress of the police commissioner's wife, a close friend of mine. I wish I could take you to her but she sews only for high-level people. Even I, a great director's wife, need intervention and mediation to get to her." When she described her things, she used French to show off more.

Her homecomings were real spectacles. Food, drinks, cookies, she brought along in fancy tin boxes, unheard of fruits people turn over in their fingers, raising their eyebrows in astonishment. Some greenish things, studded with knots like knuckles on a fist, with a delicate skin and a white, very sweet flesh that leaves you with a mouthful of hard, flat, black seeds. Another dark green cylindrical thing, the size of a big date with a sandy taste. Then that thing she calls the lawyer, l'avocat (avocado); she would pronounce the word slowly. They would peel it, eat a portion with bread, "like butter, a butter grown on trees, praise the Lord!" they would say. And they would wait for summer for these fruits of hers.

Yes, the town women looked up to her, but they also avoided her.

"She's so full of herself," they would say. "She only mixes with the rich."

"That standard is above me. No ma'm, I cannot compete. No matter what I cook, she'll still find a defect in it."

"What makes you think she'd accept your invitation, anyway? Don't you know what she did to her own sister? Her sister invited her to a lunch that left the sister in financial straits. Do you know what she did?"

"No. What did she do?"

"Well, she never showed up, because her sister is a poor woman. Have you ever heard anything like that? She simply left them waiting like dirt. If her sister's poverty is a disgrace, why did she let her borrow money and take all the trouble?"

"During the celebration of her son's birth, the sister's husband gave the woman keys in a dirty white rag, and asked her to give them to his wife. You know what she did? She lifted them with thumb and index finger, away from her face, and went in to the celebration shouting: 'Whose keys are these?' The room was full of people who mocked and laughed. 'Some people still carry their keys in rags,' she went on giggling. Then standing above her sister, she added: 'I think they're yours. Hee, hee.' And so saying, she dropped the keys and they fell in her sister's lap. The guests were amazed by her shamelessness."

"Oh my! What did she do? The sister I mean."

"Her face became pale as a ghost, and she kept wiping her forefinger below her eye."

"And what does *she* carry her keys in, gold or silver?"

"Everyone who learns two letters of French, starts treating the world as their servants."

"And lives in the capital."

"And marries a director."

"A director who rides a motorcycle and plays accordion."

"What accordion does he play? He just spreads and folds the instrument; all that comes out are cracked sounds."

"Anyway, the first time he showed up with it, people were dumbfounded. They called it the music bellows."

"No one needs to be so haughty. There's this woman from my village. She was the sheikh's wife. She couldn't speak a word of even Arabic. She used to take things from the servants with a ladle. She was so contemptuous she disdained touching the servants. Well, I lived to see her herding a cow for food alone."

"And how about the Pharaoh? What made him haughty?"

"Money."

"There you are."

"Haughtiness did exist in the time of the Prophet, God's prayer and peace be upon Him," said the daughter of the town imam and scholar. Then she recited the following Hadith: "A man entered the mosque. He looked right and left but found no place except near a poor man. He sat in it and gathered his clothes around him. 'Are you afraid that he will contaminate you with his poverty or that you will contaminate him with your wealth?' said the Prophet. 'I yield half my wealth to him,' the rich man said. 'Take what your brother gave you,' the Prophet, God's prayer and peace be upon Him, said to the poor man. 'No,' he replied, 'I'm afraid that if I become like him I'd act in the same way.'"

The visitor was visualizing her mother, her forefinger wiping her lower eyelid on the day of the celebration and the keys, when she heard the plastic slippers clacking again. The aunt came back, holding a tray on which stood a big, pink, ceramic coffee pot, striped with light green. She poured coffee with milk and sugar from the pot, handed the visitor a glass and a plate of cookies, and the latter began to chew gloomily.

The next week, a delivery boy knocked on the visitor's office door. She was bent over her papers, and when she looked up, she was face to face with her own aunt's husband. They blinked and stared at each other.

He handed her a letter in a holder. She took it and signed in a register. He folded both the folder and the register, turned away, and then drifted down the staircase without uttering a word. She sat there with her head in her hands. An office boy came in.

"The man who just walked out..." she said to him.

"You mean the Ministry of Agriculture delivery boy?"

"Is he a delivery boy then? Since when?"

"Oh!" he exclaimed, waving his hand backwards to a remote past. "Since the days of colonization."

A Hollywood Star

He was very popular in the forties, when radio began. People used to drop whatever they had in their hands and rush to listen. The minute the broadcaster announced, "Radio Maroc Presents ...," people would gather around their sets and listen attentively to the weekly dramatic performance in which he was always the star.

We did not have a radio then. Not that we could not afford it, but Grandfather stubbornly decided that he would not buy that box unless he could see the Andalusian orchestra in it. That is exactly what he said, as if he were talking about the television. Incredible indeed!

People thought my grandfather was joking or talking nonsense or simply using words to cover his greed. For how could he, for heaven's sake, see the orchestra with its chairs, violins, and lutes in a box thirty centimeters by thirty? And so on and so forth.

Grandfather had long since passed away when television began, and every time I watch it, I cannot help but be amazed by his statement of so many years ago.

I was six or seven in the fifties, when we took to going to our neighbors' house to listen to the dramatic performance on Thursday evenings. At least I think it was on Thursdays. I admired the actor's voice and what he could do with Arabic, especially in the Thousand and One Nights serial, with its fabulous atmosphere and sound effects. Since the audience was restricted to listening only, they used their imagination without limit.

I can still remember, for instance, the story of "the man whose lower part down to his feet is stone and who, from his navel up to his hair, is human, and whose moans come from the bottom of his sad liver." And I remember the maids in King Shah Zaman's Palace, their laughter mixed with the sound of water gurgling in a fountain. And descriptions of oil lamps, demons, human and jinni kings, slaves, tradesmen, fishermen, tramps, corridors, palaces, pearls, and crystals, etc.

That actor's voice and The Arabian Nights blended into one entity and made me think of him as a tall, slender, brown, good-looking young man. Then in the sixties, television began, and there he was—a small, middle-aged, ugly man. I was shaken by the shock and found myself at a loss. How could a voice like his be compatible with an image like this! So I simply disregarded those dramatic performances of his. It's true that handsome Egyptian and American movie stars might have played a part in my decision. Yet, it is what *every* woman around me did. Men, however, admired the old actor even more.

He dropped out of my memory until I began work as a journalist and set off one day to attend the rehearsal of a new play. There the actor was again, completely transformed. The skin of his face was lifeless and rigid like leather, with a paleness that some have attributed to diabetes. His back was bent and his stubbly beard was white. The rims of his watery eyes were red, and below his eyes hung swollen pockets. The few teeth he had left were darkened by alcohol. He was wearing worn jeans and, from his glorious days, a battered, green corduroy jacket with leather patches on its elbows. A black cap covered his head, though sparse white hairs did hang below his collar. He held a cheap Casasport cigarette in tobacco-stained, lean, shaking fingers, and he nodded drowsily as he waited.

When his turn came, it turned out that he had a small role, and yet, he kept stammering and stuttering until the director finally said to him in an unbelievable impertinence: "If you are in your dotage, stay home, man! This is no charity, you know." Fear came upon the old actor but not humiliation.

Was this the man who used to dominate the airwaves? I was bewildered, embarrassed, and at the same time driven by journalistic curiosity. I wanted to know what on earth could have led to this dilemma. I arranged an interview with one of the female comedians, knowing well how women, in that milieu in particular, are ready to talk about their colleagues. And so it was, that the minute I pronounced the fellow's name she burst out with this story.

"It's all the fault of that American movie. But what the hell had Hollywood to do with him? 'He who's content becomes sated and God frees him from want,' as the old saying puts it." She then mentioned the title of the movie in which he had appeared, and I remembered it. It was one of those Hollywood epics in the eighties. Our star did have an important role in it. People were dumbfounded at his performance and what Hollywood could do with talent. Rumors sprang up about him in artistic and journalistic circles, that he had come back with a Samsonite suitcase full of "cards" (the jargon for dollars), as in the movies. Other rumors circulated that he had brought back marble bath tubs and sinks, twenty-four carat gold taps, gold door-handles and phones, and that he was now living de facto an Arabian Nights lifestyle.

"Yes, yes," I said to the female comedian. "I do remember now, but where are all the dollars, gold, and marble now?"

"Heavens! There was no marble. The phones, handles, and taps were just gold-colored mineral. The Samsonite held ten thousand dollars, that's all."

"Small fortunes look extravagant in the minds of the needy, don't they? But what happened exactly?"

"Well, he came back, and the first thing he did was to resign from the radio. That was his first mistake. The second was that he started looking down on us as if we didn't know his background and what he was before."

"What was he?"

"A worker in a gas station on the road to Casablanca."

"Really? And he changed after the American movie?"

"Completely. He even began walking with a certain mannerism. My Lord! You know Namrud, the King who threw Prophet Abraham into fire? He began walking like him."

"How?"

"Quivering, swaying, beating the ground with his feet, and looking at the sky. I swear by God, the One and Only. Until I saw him, I didn't know that men pranced. Unbelievable! It was then that I knew it was all over with him."

"Yes, but what happened to the dollars?"

"I'm coming to that. His third mistake, the serious one, was to rent a suite at the Hilton Hotel and turn it into a fancy office in the American way. It cost him four thousand *dirhams*."

"Per month?"

"Per day. Good heavens! Per day, ma'm! And he hired a beautiful English-speaking secretary for a salary of five thousand dirhams, because he intended to use her as secretary and interpreter. Smart, huh!"

"By the way, he doesn't speak any English. How could he perform with the Americans?"

"They made him memorize the words, and he repeated them without understanding. Crazy! So anyway, the guy was now an international star, but he could hardly receive agents in his dilapidated house in the old medina. The house is across Buqrun Alley with its heaps of potatoes, tomatoes, onions, and sardines, its dirt, sewage water, and drains crammed with rubbish....

"And to add to the pomp, he bought a luxurious car and hired a driver. He began wearing the expensive suits he had purchased in New York, sitting in the splendid office, and waiting for the phone to ring. But nothing happened." She wiped her hands and was seized by a laugh that went on and on. The satisfaction, which had been in her face and tone of voice and was now so obviously overt, made me angry. Then she wiped her tears, gave a groan of ecstatic pleasure, and went on:

"A month later the show was over, and everything came to an end, the office, the car, the secretary, the driver, the dollars, and the man himself. He was gone. Only his empty frame remained, like a hollow palm tree."

A Genius Filmmaker

He came back home with the film he had made for his graduation from a prestigious French cinema school. A great film. Best writing, best photography, best music, best direction, best everything. Let alone the story, the dialogue, and the acting.

The examination committee's report called him a "genius" and stated that he had reached a level far exceeding professionals. The minister of home affairs, in an address to the government film directors, said: "There you are. He is working with less money and under more difficult conditions than you are. Look what he's done. What's the matter with you?"

The press called him "the genius filmmaker," following the report of the French examination committee. It also described his film as a "specific shift." For the first time, critics forgot their inclination to view all films with contempt and gave the man praise and glory.

"The critics too!" we all exclaimed in disbelief. "Wow!"

I did not hear a word of calumny except for one. I heard an Algerian man say at the end of the show: "When that boy broke into those gasps, I wanted to walk up to him with a handkerchief. Why do Moroccans love stretching out a scene so much? If an actor in a Moroccan film so much as turns away, the camera will follow him right up to the top of the street." The man gave the type of scornful chuckle I hate.

In addition to the film and the certificate, he brought back a French wife. She had also graduated from the same cinema school, but she chose to work as a secretary for some multinational company to insure a secure income so that the genius could dedicate himself to his talent. People were bewildered. They could not understand how a European woman would make a sacrifice of that magnitude.

His second film came out two years later. Another piece of art. At that time a foreign producer asked me to suggest a good local filmmaker to direct a documentary she wanted to produce on Moroccan folklore. I said to myself: "Moroccans are accused of fighting new talent. Now an opportunity has come right to the door. Why not take it? On one hand, you'll do good and, on the other, you'll prove that Moroccans will support new talent when it's deserved."

I got hold of the genius filmmaker's address, phone number, and the clips of articles about him that had appeared in the Francophone press. I mailed all this to the producer with an enthusiastic letter, advising her to sign a contract at once. I ended the letter with this phrase: "Just trust me and one day you'll thank me."

Sometime later she sent me the following letter:

"That 'genius' (she mentioned his name) has ruined me. I have sold my house and my car to pay for this film. He said universities would buy the documentary, and I believed him. Do you know how many I sold? Four. Four copies only. Where is that genius you were talking about? What he did is rubbish, worthless rubbish."

She continued, "Don't try advising people. That is my advice. I include a copy of that thing he calls 'documentary,' so you can see for yourself the amount of harm you have caused me. I will never forgive you."

She did not even make the effort to sign the letter. I was stupefied. I intended to pay her back twofold, as the Arab saying puts it, if not a little more, but God gave me patience. I said to myself: "Let's see that damn documentary first."

I put the video in the VCR. I sat down to watch, but what I saw made me forget the letter, myself, and the world around me. The whole film consisted of talking heads, as they call them; they seemed to be reading from books. Some were in fact reading from hidden papers. Readymade, flat expressions like the speech of politicians. Dead shots, like photos on white-walled rooms, a few roofs, nothing else. No movement, no scenery, no apparent technique, no editing, no music, no directing, no nothing. It was as if a child had turned a camera on and begun shooting things at random.

The video ended, the screen darkened and started hissing annoyingly, but I was unable to reach the remote control. When I came to, I found myself uttering that Moroccan saying that I had never agreed with before: "Not doing a good deed won't do you any harm."

"How could this have happened?" I said, wiping my hands in despair, "This is crazy."

Oh God, what have movies to do with me? Why didn't I just mind my own business and spare myself this humiliation? But what good were my questions now? I reexamined the situation and saw that I deserved all that had happened to me. I found that I had caused the woman's ruin who, were it not for God's grace, could have taken me to court. Lawyers would have no problem finding reasons for a suit. I could hear them saying things like:

"Due to the fact that it is nonsensical that a person would leave her work and spend her time assisting others,

"Due to the fact that it is nonsensical that a person would praise non-existent qualifications,

"Due to this and due to that, it is a case of robbery and fraud with premeditation."

I took the receiver and began dialing, but I could not face my friend. I feared complications, as the disaster was still fresh. I confined myself to a letter of regret and apology. Then I said to myself out loud: "I vow to God that I will never recommend a soul, even if it were my own mother."

The subject was finished, and so was my relationship with the woman. It would not survive what I had done and what she had said, which remained, as it was, making me feel guilty and weighing like a stone in my chest every time I thought about it.

So, I tried to find an explanation for the disaster. But I found only more accounts of other equally bad movies by that guy, and I heard that he had separated from his wife. But how could his separation from his wife destroy all his talent?

Then, I happened to go to a bakery that had opened in a remote neighborhood and was the talk of the town. A line of customers waited up to the end of the street, but the line was moving fast. Salesgirls, like nurses in white coats and white head covers, stood behind a glass counter, putting the bread in plastic bags. I reached the cashier, and who was the cashier but our guy himself: yes, the "genius filmmaker."

I hurried out, not knowing if I had picked up my change or not. So, it was he who had opened that bakery! He took people's money and returned their change, leaving it in a stone saucer with an air of melancholy, despite his sumptuous gray suit and pink tie.

Now my need to solve the puzzle of the "genius filmmaker" became a matter of life and death. One day I came across one of the cameramen who used to work with him. I asked him about the guy and mentioned the ill-fated documentary. I sensed he was sympathetic, so I asked him directly.

"How do you explain the differences?"

"I don't know," he said, touching his cheek hesitantly. "I don't know if I should tell you. You'll find what I'll say hard to believe."

My curiosity increased as he said, "Remember the two films that caused all that tumult?"

"Yes, what about them?"

"Well, he didn't direct them."

"Who did?"

"His wife did."

"I don't believe it."

"I told you. Truth sometimes is unbelievable. I wouldn't have believed it myself if I had not been there. Yes, his wife is the creator of his films."

"And the graduation certificate? Is that also a fraud?"

He nodded and raised his eyebrows.

"She accepted? She consented? She could look him in the eyes every morning?"

"She handed him genius, benevolently, just as she handed him his livelihood."

"Like handing to others one's own children."

"It's a special species of love."

"A clumsy one. But how about divorce then?"

"It came in, when love stepped out."

"She refused to continue the game."

"Or was perhaps disgusted by it. Who knows? She did wake up. That's what's important."

Her Best Friend

When Khadduje was a girl, Amina, who lived next door, was her best friend. The two girls learned dressmaking from the same woman. In those days, there were no schools for girls. There was only the sewing teacher and, for a playground, the street itself.

Khadduje loved her friend better than her sisters Zuhur and Shama. Back then, neighbors were close to kin, and neighbors knew everything about each other. Khadduje and Amina's friendship became even closer in adulthood, because they married two brothers. Their weddings were celebrated on the same night, and they lived in the same house.

In those days, a young bride stayed in her husband's house away from the eyes of strange men. She was so concerned about concealing herself from men that she almost "wore a face veil to feed the rooster," to quote a popular saying. Khadduje and Amina's friendship helped them through that kind of life. They shared the daily chores of washing clothes, cleaning the house, cooking, kneading the bread dough, and sewing, from the moment in the morning when their father-in-law wrapped his head up in his turban and left with his two sons for the family shop.

As for the mother-in-law, she just sat. She sat and did not stop complaining: "The food is burning." "The coffee is flowing over." "What's that stain in the bottom of the cooking pot? You can see yourself in the neighbor's pots." Bla, bla, bla. That was when she did not moan and groan and try to look as if she were dying, calling on her mother and her limbs: "Oh my mother!" "Oh my head!" "Oh my hand!" "Oh my foot!" And with that kind of atmosphere, the family ate their daily meals.

Khadduje armed herself with patience, with the support of her friend Amina, and her sister Shama, who often visited her, bringing news of the street. Khadduje's husband was very nice to Shama. He always asked her to stay for dinner and accompanied her back home. He even brought her from the family shop a bath towel that Shama, renowned for being fond of delicate fabrics, still keeps in the bottom of her trunk. It was a breathtaking pink towel, interwoven with white

41

thread and bordered on both ends with streaks of faded green and white supple fringes.

At the end of the first year of marriage, Khadduje gave birth to a boy and Amina to a girl. Only then were they allowed to visit their parents.

At the entrance to her street, Khadduje looked with longing at the worn stone houses with their wall of peeling paint. She was suddenly back in the past. All sorts of images and events, quarrels, joys, and grief, came tumbling into her mind. When she saw the iron grill at the window above the front door of her family house, she remembered how, as a child, she used to grasp the sill and swing back and forth.

The first turn was always Shama's. Khadduje remembered how she and Amina would lift Shama. When she reached the sill and grasped it, they would push her back and forth, and Shama's dark, thick plaits would fly through the air, and her earring stones would bump against her small face.

Khadduje saw once more Shama's pale tan, her delicate nose, her dark radiant eyes, and the gold bracelets on her wrist. Her sleeves would be rolled up and her well-fitting, elegant dress would hang down. Zuhur and she had no earrings, no bracelets, no elegant dresses, only old shifts wearing out on their bodies.

She was surprised that she had not noticed the injustice of such a treatment before. But she pushed the idea out of her head and thought instead of the time when her husband had become ill, when the family was leaving for the spring outing to the country. Shama had offered to take care of him so that Khadduje would not miss the outing. A gesture for which she was grateful, though Zuhur too had offered to help and stayed with Shama. Then she thought of that bizarre incident that had taken place at the time, an incident that was related in the family circle for a long time to come.

On the first evening of the two sisters' attendance to the sick man, Shama's screams rose in one of the rooms. Zuhur rushed in and found her sister trembling and pointing under a bed. When she bent down to look, she saw a coiled serpent and scampered off, running through the streets without even a piece of cloth to cover her head. When she reached home, she swore that she would not set foot in that house again for as long as she lived.

What turned out to be bizarre about the incident was this: The serpent was dead. It had come in with the load of firewood. Their father had killed it, and it turned out that Shama had simply brought the snake along to scare her sister away. This only confirmed Shama's daring nature. After all, she was the first girl in town to pluck her eyebrows and cut her front hair in bangs.

All this went through Khadduje's mind as she crossed the threshold of her old house and looked up at the windowsill above. Inside, the house seemed different. The central court and the doors appeared smaller, the rooms more humble, the ceilings lower, as if the whole structure had shrunk.

A week later whispers were heard up and down the street that the mother-in-law had taken Amina back and left Khadduje to stay at her family's home. Apprehension seized the family, but they kept silent until the mother burst out at her husband: "You see that old witch?"

"Hold your tongue," he replied. "We don't know yet what they're up to."

"Can't you see what they're up to? I'm sure the old witch is rummaging through our girl's room at this very moment. And you're sitting here, saying: 'We don't know what they're up to.'"

"What's the rush for?"

"You'd rather sit and wait for the worst to happen. Wake up, man. Go find out. Send a mediator. Do something."

"They'll come without mediation."

But they did not come. Instead, a delivery boy for the law court showed up with Khadduje's repudiation paper. Her husband had divorced her. Her mother wailed and then praised her daughter, and the neighborhood women echoed her sobs: "We accepted trash and the trash rejected us!"

"They'll be sorry, I'm telling you, for they'll never find the likes of Khadduje."

"Yes, but the ultimate defeat, my friend, is to be discarded and thrown back to one's own family."

"May such scum be defeated by life."

"If I had only known what kind of people they were," cried the mother.

"Don't blame yourself. It's not your fault."

"That husband seemed such a good fellow. Why, he looked like he wouldn't disturb a hen sitting on its eggs."

"Who said that husbands don't change?"

"May God revenge you, Khadduje, you're such an enduring soul."

"Yes."

"She worked like a slave and was always polite."

"I know."

"They sent her on a visit to her family and followed her with the repudiation."

"They were up to wickedness all the time."

"And they couldn't find a single fault with her."

"No."

"Or a pretext."

"They don't need pretexts."

"What kills me, my friends, is that old witch is rejoicing. She begat boys and I girls. 'A boy is a glory even if he were to lie dead in a tomb,' she said to my face."

"Enough!" Khadduje's father shouted, striding out and casting his djellabah over his shoulder.

"He's right. Wailing won't change anything!"

From that moment, Khadduje began to feel that she was not in her proper place. She was embarrassed when the baby cried or when she took the soap to wash his diapers or when she stretched out her hand to eat the family food. It seemed as though after she married, thorns had grown in her place. She felt guilty, as if she had committed the ultimate sin when her husband repudiated her.

"People are talking," her mother said one day, her tone hard. "They won't shut up until you marry again."

"But what I got from the first marriage, I'll get from the second."

"Not all people are the same."

"But what chance do I have to marry, a woman who has been repudiated, who has a child and no good looks?"

"There're buyers for all kinds of grain."

"And how about luck? Where am I to get it?"

"Were it for sale, we would have bought it. Were it for rent, we would have rented it."

"What do we have to buy it with?" asked Khadduje.

"You might have luck yet," said the mother.

"When the first husband came, you said you would have plenty of silk to wear."

"But I didn't get one ounce of sugar from him," said the mother.

"And I got a repudiation paper. Why?"

"Keeping secrets is sometimes merciful."

"What do you mean?" asked Khadduje. "Mother?"

"Nothing. Enough now. You're giving me a headache."

"You really think I'll find a new husband?"

"Yes, if God wills it."

Saying that, the mother wet her fingertip and rubbed it on the wall as if fingerprinting her words.

"How?"

"Some man will return from a long absence or will lose his present wife and need a new one."

It was as if the doors of heaven had opened and let in the mother's statement. For no sooner was the baby weaned than Khadduje was married off to a civil servant working for the Ministry of Home Affairs, a good man who wanted children.

As the mother packed Khadduje's trunk, a trunk covered with light blue cloth fastened with iron studs, she said: "Remember, you can't lead any man by his ear." She lifted her chin sideways and touched her earlobe in a warning gesture. "Stay in your house, my girl, and watch out. I'll keep your gold jewelry here. I'll put it in my trunk. Stay away from the neighbors and chance acquaintances. And, above all, trust no woman, even if she were the daughter of your own mother."

"The daughter of my own mother?"

"Yes. And behave as if your father could see you. Take after your mother. Have you ever seen me flirting with shopkeepers or selling from your father's wheat, olives, or oil behind his back, like some wives do? Well, have you?"

"No, Mother."

"Be patient, no matter what. What else can I say? Remember my words. May my blessing be with you. May God keep envious people and sorcerers away from you, as he kept the elephant from the gates of Mecca. Say Amen! And I also packed in your trunk a beautiful new piece of fabric."

It was the worst day in Khadduje's life, when she left the baby sleeping, early one grey morning, and walked behind the new husband to the bus station and hence to Rabat.

For the next thirty years, she did as her mother had told her. She stayed in her house and trusted no woman. She did visit her hometown when her husband took vacations, and she came on happy and sad occasions in the family. Each time she came, she brought loads of presents for everyone, especially her friend Amina.

On one visit, when both friends were old, Khadduje stayed overnight with Amina. They went to bed, and as soon as they lay down, Khadduje said in the dark: "Now that the mother-in-law has passed away, you're free at last, my friend."

"What good is freedom when my life is over? But you, thank God, you've enjoyed freedom for a long time."

"Me? It was a spoiled one."

"Why?"

"My child. They took him away from me. Didn't you know?"

"Yes, but God has rewarded you with many gorgeous children, hasn't He? Plus a home of your own, where no old woman lords it over you."

"And given me a life away from home," Khadduje went on. "And loneliness."

"Angels are with you. And God, my friend."

"Don't you realize what it's been like? Months passed without a soul visiting me. Sometimes, I lost track of the days and nearly forgot how to speak."

"No one has everything, and you rest at ease. Don't you?"

"No. No ease. Not a day passed when I didn't ask myself why I was repudiated. And I will never be at ease until I know. What did I do wrong? What's the answer?" Khadduje asked. Amina remained silent.

"What is it?"

"Won't you stop asking that question?"

"No, not until I know the answer."

Amina cleared her voice but did not utter a word.

"You're the only one left who could possibly know," Khadduje insisted, "and if I die before I know it, I won't be able to forgive you.

Please Amina, in the name of our friendship, love, and companionship. In the name of kinship, the bread and salt...."

"OK. OK. I'll tell you."

They pushed their blankets off and sat up in bed.

"Your first husband," Amina began, "had an affair.... Oh my goodness!"

"With whom?"

"Your sister. Shama. There it is. Now, are you satisfied? Why in the hell did you want to hear this?"

Khadduje did not answer. She felt cold and dizzy. She embraced her knees, buried her face, and sobbed. After a long and heavy silence, Amina went on: "He said to your father, 'I want to repudiate Khadduje and marry Shama,' but your father refused, bless his soul."

After another long silence, Khadduje asked in distress: "Did Shama want to marry him?"

"I'm telling you she had an affair with him. Of course she wanted to marry him, but your father was against it. He was like a fish bone in her throat."

"My own sister? Oh God! Why?"

"Some're like that."

"The whore! 'Trust no woman even if she were the daughter of your own mother.' So that's what my mother meant. And I didn't feel, didn't see, didn't hear, didn't get it. They were playing around, but I was blind to it."

The friends were silent, and Khadduje spent the night staring into darkness. When she went back to Rabat, staring became a habit. Her body was in her house, but her mind was back home, and images popped up one after the other: Shama's visits! Her former husband asking her to stay for dinner, then accompanying her home! The towel! His sudden illness during the spring outing and her sister's offer to nurse him! The serpent! Oh God! What a sad mind! What a vile couple made of the same substance!

Khadduje would sometimes be overwhelmed by distress. She would slip her hands out of the bread dough or laundry suds, raise them to the sky and plead: "Oh God, You who listen to those who are longing, who enact justice and come to the relief of those who're in sorrow, by our Lord Mohamed who's paved the way to You, tear my sister up as she's torn my baby away from me!"

That year colonialism ended, the French left, and Khadduje's husband was promoted to be the governor of a southern district. But neither the improvement in her position nor the move, nor the change of place and way of life, could ease Khadduje's mind. The instant she woke, she was overcome by feelings of strangeness, horror, and fear, all combining to make her lose interest in life.

When she had settled down in her new mansion, her friend Amina came to visit, together with her husband and her grown daughter. Khadduje rejoiced when she saw her friend, after having forgotten what rejoicing feels like. But Amina was tense and began packing almost as soon as she had arrived.

"What're you doing?" Khadduje asked. "You've not yet cleaned off the dust of the road. Are you already fed up with us?"

"We don't want to be burdensome guests."

"You're not a guest. And it's your first visit. I swear...."

"Don't swear, please. Because I'm not staying, really."

"Weren't you planning to visit the shrine of Mulay Ali Al-Sharif? What's gotten into you, all of a sudden?"

Amina's face turned pale. Khadduje saw a strange glitter in her eyes and glances, which did not seem her own. Apprehension and puzzlement filled Khadduje suddenly. She tried awkwardly to take the suitcase away. Amina clung to it, and the two of them stood there pulling it back and forth.

"Let go," yelled Amina.

"I will not before I know the reason. There must be some reason."

"It's your husband."

"My husband? What about him?"

"My husband went to see him and all he had to say was 'goodbye.' He didn't even pretend to have us stay longer."

When her husband came home, Khadduje said to him: "What's going on between you and my friend's husband? He comes and you say: 'goodbye'?"

"Why should I not say it?"

"After all the distance they traveled? My best friend comes to visit me for the first time and we are not even polite. What a shame! Wait till the neighbors hear about it."

"They have traveled a long way, it's true, but I'm not sure she's your best friend."

"She is, upon my word," she said, blinking.

He said, "That best friend of yours, you see, came to offer her daughter to me, like a commodity." Khadduje screwed up her eyes, trying to concentrate. "She sent her husband over to my office to say: 'We'd like to propose our daughter to you in marriage. We want no dowry. We just want the honor of a relationship with you.' 'Is it with me or with the governor?' I asked. 'What's the difference?' he retorted. 'And what about Khadduje?' I asked again. 'Come on,' he replied. 'Khadduje has become old and decrepit. Leave her to her prayer and enjoy your life. My daughter is young, beautiful, educated, and modern. She's the wife you need for your important position.' Such a dull idiot! I could hear his wife speaking through his mouth."

Khadduje did not bury her face in her knees this time and sob. Her lips parted and she gazed silently at her husband. A heavy tiredness crept over her and pressed her shoulders down.

The Trade Unionist

He heard a catfight. Sharp yowls and cries. It is ten p.m. He lit a cigarette, placed it between his lips and began coding in a number on the remote control of his television. Children appeared on the screen, pelting Israeli soldiers in military vehicles and tanks. Then a hole in a ceiling, crossed by bent iron bars, through which the sky was visible. A woman beside a pile of rubble looked at the hole and complained to the camera. But he could not tell whether this was the West Bank or Baghdad.

He coded in another number. An old man stood in a building with demolished sides. More debris showed on the screen, and a woman said in a Palestinian accent: "They've demolished my house. They've swept it away."

"May God demolish them and those who're empowering them! Amen!" he said and pushed in new numbers on the remote control until a similar pile of rubble lying in front of huge leafy trees appeared on the screen. A big American stood beside it and said: "My house is demolished. The wind lifted it up and smashed it against the ground. All in less than a second."

"No need for rakes," he said in front of the screen. "Houses go down, but the trees stand up to the wind."

He pushed in new numbers on the remote control until a singer from the Gulf countries appeared. She was surrounded by a bunch of women with loose, long hair. Then his Emir appeared, investing a man with a decoration.

"Honestly, His Royal Highness, may God protect him, does support and encourage us," said the singer to a Lebanese journalist who answered: "Indeed. Do you have a strategy for your work?"

"Yes of course."

"What is it?"

"Our strategy is universality."

"You mean, you want the world to listen to your music? Isn't that a little pretentious?"

"We have done it in the Arab countries. Why not the world?"

He shook his head with an ironic grin and turned the TV off. He got to his feet, made a round of the windows, and locked them securely. The catfight had stopped. He went to the kitchen and turned on the tap, and the pipe gurgled forth a stream of water. He splashed some in his face. Water poured into the sink and dripped through the drain into a bucket below. He went to the bookcase, began to pull out novels and poetry collections, read the titles, and pushed the books back.

"From detention to politics, to history, to libertinism, obscenity, and odiousness," he murmured to himself, turning away and adding: "These so-called modern writers even tried attacks on God. TV is a nuisance. Books are a bore. What time is it?" he asked. "Eleven," he answered.

He pulled up a chair, stood on it, and reached a box-shaped plastic file on the top shelf. Suddenly, dogs barked outside. He trembled. The chair shook beneath him. Papers and photographs poured out of the file, and he fell forward on his face.

He sat up with difficulty, sensed a headache, and felt stiff joints and pain all over his body. The leather of the chair was ripped. And he heard a noise outside.

"Goddam you sons of thieves!" he said in a trembling, low voice, gathering himself up and limping toward the window. He pressed his face against the shutter, suddenly frightened. Peeping through the cracks, he saw torchlight swaying from side to side on the unpaved road. He heard footsteps, horses clip-clopping, and the rattle of a cart. He stood by the shutter until the sounds receded and the dogs became quiet.

Then he turned from the window, pulling on his lower lip with a loose, shaking hand.

"So this is the retirement you were dreaming of!" he muttered.

He passed a mirror and looked in it, apprehensively. A bent back, a skinny body, a white stub of a beard, frightened eyes with dark yellow pouches below, a deathly pallor, pimples covering the left cheek.

He did not want to look at his eyes directly. His fear increased and he walked away, shuffling in his slippers, putting his hands on the walls for support. He went to the kitchen and forgot suddenly why he had come there.

"What am I here for?" he asked, touching his white hair. He opened the refrigerator and took out a bottle of water, but it slipped from his hands and shattered on the floor. He stood there, his loose hand still in the shape of the grasp; then he walked out, stepping on the water and broken glass.

He gathered the papers and photographs and went into the bedroom, avoiding the mirror. He put the papers and photos on the bed and sat down, tucking a cigarette between his lips. He struck a match and brought it up, sheltered in his hands. The flame lit up his face and the cracks between his fingers, but he could not manage to light the cigarette.

He spat it out and put the match in an ashtray. He felt a stiffness in his left shoulder and cramps in his hip and his chest, cutting his breath. So that fall still has consequences, he thought. It was midnight now and the cats had resumed their wailing.

"You stood up to the forces of repression, but now a handful of peasants is scaring the hell out of you?" he said to himself. "You? The powerful unionist who spent your life in demonstrations, rallies, sit-ins, detention camps, and torture rooms. You are finished. Look at you! In one year you have become prey to fear, sorrow, fatigue, and cowardice. They're looting your harvest, and you're peeping out of your hole, like a rat."

He was overcome by a fit of coughing. It shook him, choked him, tore his lungs, and left him panting with a rattle in his throat. Then the cough left him like a dropped rag.

It is two a.m. His breathing has returned to normal. He took the old papers, put them on his knees, and began looking back at the past. May Day, 1960. "Do you know, comrades, that two-thirds of the national income go to one-fourth of the population? Our first aim, therefore, is to reach a fair distribution of the national income." He heard applause and singsong acclamations. The streaming banners carried by thousands of people in the Casablanca soccer stadium flashed through his mind: "Workers are fired but thieves are protected!" "Unionists in jails. Where're the rights? Where's the law?"

An image of the famous raised-fist emblem coalesced in his mind, as did the following slogans: Employers. Dictatorship. The enemy.

Our Central Syndicate. Workers' liberation. Demonstration. Protest. Struggle....

"Comrades, we all share one thing. Life is full of convulsions, but there are those who are convulsed with indigestion and those who're convulsed with starvation. Our second aim, therefore, is raising wages." Applause and acclamation burst out in his mind again. "If there is food, let everyone eat from it, says a Chinese proverb.

"Some will ask: 'How?' Well, I'll tell them how. By raising taxes. By taking from the rich and giving to the poor. By supplying workers and peasants with health care, education, machines, and tractors. By cooperation and solidarity. By abolishing selfishness and individualism.

"Thus the poor will be rich, love will be whole, and a new progressive, open society will develop instead of this reactionary, impervious-to-innovation society we have today."

"You were dreaming with your eyes wide open, and people applauded you," he said to himself. "Take from the rich and give to the poor, to unify love? Well, you're doing that now, aren't you? You're paying for their health and social security. You take them to private clinics. You treat them as equals. Where's that love? They even steal the food from your kitchen."

He put down the papers and picked up a black and white photograph of himself as a young man. He is delivering another speech. The wind is blowing his dark hair back, ruffling the sides of his jacket. On the back of the picture is the following inscription: "Casablanca. May Day, 1985." He lifts the photo in his tobacco-stained fingers. "That's you, a man with an issue," he says to himself, "for which you'd cross seven oceans, the Arabian desert, and come back with a hundred red she-camels.

"That was the day you said in a speech that the parliamentary deputy who does not even attend the assembly meetings and accepts three million centimes wages at the end of the month is serving nothing but his own interest.

"The 'respectable' deputy who does not even show up in meetings gets three million centimes, but the worker who toils from sunrise to sunset gets three.

"What're we paying them three millions for? What the hell are they doing for us? Do you know, comrades, how many jobs can be created out of the deputies' salaries? And the salaries of the government?

"You went even further. You called the ministers thieves. You paid for that word with jail time. You have fallen apart in those long detentions and haven't been able to change anything. You were punched, slapped on the face, you had your mother cursed, your ancestors insulted, and you still couldn't change anything. For the sake of workers. Workers? Those workers are now robbing you. They are taking your benefits and capital and leaving you with taxes and payments for irrigation.

"Why didn't I stay at home? I have got to find a way out. Fear is going to kill me if the coughing does not. What time is it now?"

It is four a.m. The catfight has stopped and he has not noticed. He thought for a moment, despondent, and then smiled. He looked relieved. He looked as if he now knew what to do.

"Go get some rest," he said to the light as he turned it off, his smile spreading over his face. Then he lay face down, groaning in comfort, his arms dangling on each side of the bed. Before long he was snoring.

He woke up at eleven in the morning and went out. He got into the car, started it, and returned. He packed a suitcase, put it in the trunk of the car, got in, and drove away.

"You're leaving it to them. Aren't you?" he said to himself as he crossed the gate. "They've managed to kick you out." Yet he felt a sensation of freedom. When he reached the paved road, he pressed the accelerator and began singing with the radio.

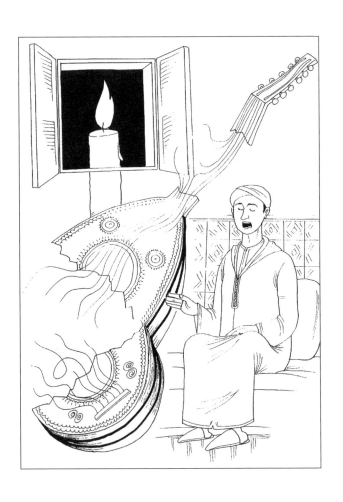

Abderrahim

The protagonist of this story is my mother's cousin, Abderrahim. In my mind, he is sixteen or seventeen. I do not know exactly. I have always envisioned him as a fair, skinny, delicate young man, with a thin djellabah, a soft turban, and lemon-yellow slippers. But this is a completely made-up portrait that does not exist in my mother's story. I think my sense of his fragility is a result of the tragic incidents of the boy's life and the pain that comes over my mother's voice and countenance when she speaks of him and the name itself: "Abderrahim." The first part of it suggests submission in Arabic, and the second, when spoken, resounds like a moan.

Since he was, like my mother, his father's eldest child, and since his father and my mother's father, the two brothers, had celebrated their weddings the same night, he must be about my mother's age, and this story must have taken place in the thirties.

I also assume that he was a blacksmith apprentice, as this trade had been in the family ever since their ancestors came out from Andalusia. They were blacksmiths and also skillful farmers. This was quite common knowledge, and my mother never had to mention it when she told the boy's story. What she stressed was Abderrahim's passion for singing. "When I say passion I mean Pa-ss-ion." The term was decisive indeed. "The heart of the matter" was, as my mother put it in a reproachful tone to destiny, that Abderrahim had been mistakenly born in Morocco rather than Egypt. Had he been born in Egypt, he would, she believed, have been a famous singer like Mohamed Abdelwahab or, why not, would have had a significant presence in Arab music.

Abderrahim performed Melhun songs, singing poetry in the vernacular. He was good-looking and had a beautiful voice. Listening to him, the public was transported, the arena flamed with delight, and coins poured down on the stage from women who chanted: "Prayer and peace be upon the Messenger of God! There is no glory save that of our Lord Mohamed! May God be with that supreme glory!" Their joyful ululations followed. He became so popular that people started to pay him in advance and set their wedding dates according to his schedule.

"But winds don't blow according to the desire of the boats," my mother would say in classical Arabic, dragging her words. Then she would sigh and go back to her vernacular, wondering what on earth would have happened if the winds had blown according to the desire of the boats. In speaking of winds, she was alluding to her uncle, Abderrahim's father.

The father waited for Abderrahim one summer night, let him in, and yelled: "So now you come back home? At dawn, like a cabaret singer! Enemy of God! Your ancestors spent the night in prayer, but you spend it in debauchery!"

"Religion is not gloom, Father? And the companions of the prophet ..."

"Were there singers among the companions of the prophet? Of course not. Our ancestors left us no land or property, but they bequeathed us honor, and I will not let you soil it. I will not let you destroy your sisters' future. You, the shame of our family! You cabaret singer!" Then he went on to say that he was beginning to doubt that the boy was his legitimate son.

Stunned by his father's insult in calling him a cabaret singer, Abderrahim did not fully comprehend his father's warning to behave or else he would damn him till doomsday. As he remained speechless, the father said: "Well! What do you say?"

"Perhaps ..."

"You say perhaps, bastard!" And bubbling with anger, like a cooking pot, the father rushed to the kitchen and came back with a knife. He snatched the lute from Abderrahim's hands, chopped its strings, and smashed it against the wall so violently that only the remains of the strings were left hanging.

But the boy bought another lute, which he kept with a member of the band, and went on accepting jobs. One evening as he was singing at a wedding, he saw his father coming toward him, trampling on the sitting guests. He stopped in the middle of a song, his lips still parted. The father reached him, snatched the turban off his head, threw it over his neck, and dragged him out into the streets where some shopkeepers bent forward to look and a few passersby stopped to ask questions or to intercede or simply to watch. Those who tried to release the boy out of a religious duty or to urge the father to at least loosen his grip were totally ignored.

At home, he flung him into the first room on the right side of the ground floor, where the boy sank down, as limp as a rag. The father slammed the door, drove the bolt firmly home, and swore that he would lock up his wife and his daughters as well if they dared to open it.

For two days, Abderrahim lay in that locked room, still and silent. My mother went several times a day to ask for news, but she only found women visitors buzzing with talk and the mother and sisters weeping.

The third day, she was there when her uncle finally announced that the boy was lost at any rate, he did not want to be held responsible for his death, and they could open that door since he was already dead for him. The weeping turned into ululations of joy. The mother and the daughters rushed toward the father and kissed his hands, over and over.

My mother said that she had a feeling that universal order was overturned, after all, that winds were blowing according to the desire of the boats. She felt this especially when she saw the father talking to his son and ordering him to get ready to go to the orchard the next day, because it was their turn to irrigate the land.

Overjoyed, Abderrahim could not sleep. When the call for the dawn prayer was raised, he jumped out of bed, did his ablutions, put on his work clothes, and sat waiting for his father's call. Father and son performed their prayer side by side at the mosque, and off they went across the fields, the father with a bag slung over his shoulder.

When they got to the orchard, the father shut the gate. He pulled a rope out of his bag and tied the boy to a mulberry tree. Then he rolled up his sleeves, spat in his palms, seized a club from the top of the tree trunk, and started hitting the boy randomly. The first stroke fell on his head, but Abderrahim did not scream or call for help. The father thought that the boy did this out of spite, and so he increased his strokes, breathing hard as though he were hitting dry corn.

When he exhausted himself, he put the club down and untied Abderrahim, who collapsed, bent over, and fell unconscious to the ground. And the father went along to his work, leaving his son to wake up at his leisure.

At the end of the day, the boy was still in the same place.

"Up! Bastard!" shouted the father "On your feet and stop acting!" But Abderrahim did not get up, so the father took the club down from the tree and turned him over on his back. What lay before him was a lifeless body.

That is the point in this story where my mother always came to a stop, as if it were a normal sort of ending, as if to say: "A son was disobedient and a father punished him." Yes, there was grief in her voice but no incrimination. She did not even say how he took the body back home. On the she-donkey's back I suppose, face downwards, the head on one side and the legs on the other. Nor did she mention how he faced up to himself, the community, the mother and her daughters. These were the helpless beings to which she never gave a name, a feature, a word, or a movement, except for their weeping of course, the ululations, and the kissing of the father's hands, over and over.

Her approach irritated me, and I reacted to it with indignation. This made her stop, and I subsided in mute disapproval.

Were it my story, I would send the father to jail or at least make him sink in depression. I would not tell the story the way my mother did in the first place. I would bring in more of what she left out and put some firmness and color into the character of that boy, in contrast to his slackness and paleness in my mother's version. I would make him sturdy and bronzed from his labor at the workshop and in the fields. I would start by changing his name; I would call him "Abdelaziz," for instance. I would have him reject the father's tyranny, and I would give the women some presence in the scene, the mother at any rate. She would certainly have a say in that boy's destiny. He is her son, for heaven's sake!

I would take the story further, until old age and disease came to the father. I would see him sitting cross-legged in the corner, a brazier in front of him, for it is winter, and that year the cold is excessive. The girls have married and left home, the mother has passed away, only the son Abderrahim is still there. He would by this time be his father's age when the father had killed him under the mulberry tree. "When he died," my mother would have corrected. Abderrahim would go on with his singing and his labor in the workshop and in the orchard. He would care for his father as if he were one of his children. Because, in my version of the story, he is now married and has four children. His eldest, like his father's was, is a boy, sixteen or seventeen years old. More than that, Abderrahim would yield to the old father's whim to get him a wife.

This young man was constantly on my mind. I imagined the father really very old now, walking slowly, slowly. I imagined his loneliness in the large, cold, and empty house. No grandchildren, no Abderrahim, no nothing, as it is in reality. All he has left is delirium: "Abderrahim tied up to the mulberry tree." "Falling, bent over to the ground." "He pushes and turns him over." "The body is on the she-donkey's back, face downward." "He rolls up his sleeves and spits in his palms." "The club on the top of the tree trunk." That club! He would not possibly have kept it. He could not have absorbed all that tragedy so naturally. He must have been traumatized. He must have suffered, regretted. Deep inside, he must have regretted his actions and must now blame himself.

Were I actually to go to their town, it would be exactly as I have imagined it. I would know my way to the house. I would push the right side panel of the door that is always kept ajar. I would go into the room where Abderrahim was locked up and I would find the old man there against the wall in the dark and in the freezing cold, a brazier in front of him, which contained nothing but cold ashes.

Phone Call

"Peace be upon you!"

"And peace, God's mercy and grace be upon you!"

"Thank you, sir, for having the kindness to listen to me. And since it's a long distance call, I'll get into the subject right away. My problem is that I can't seem to keep relationships going."

"Why?"

"Because I'm lovable."

"What do you mean?"

"The people I deal with, sooner or later get attached to me. Most of the time it's later."

"What's the problem?"

"I'm continuously changing my grocer, greengrocer, upholsterer, my druggist, and so on and so forth."

"Is the problem in the market?"

"And at the work place and in the neighborhood. I keep moving from one work place to another and changing my phone number.

"Do you feel lonely?"

"Not at all. Loneliness for me is a spiritual retreat."

"How old are you?"

"Sixty."

"Try to find an occupation with old people then."

"I did. When I was a student, I knew a European couple in their eighties."

"Good idea, because the disparities between you and them will solve the problem."

"It was so obvious, it just happened without premeditation. I appreciated the wife's life away from home at her age, her vitality, cheerfulness, contentment, along with her refined taste, skill, and education. There was always a touch of beauty on and around her, a proper and becoming hairstyle, well-cut clothes, lilies in polygonal glass vases, roses in sculptured white porcelain containers, etc. Even her kitchen was a work of art. When I asked her, 'Why the kitchen?' she said: 'That's where women spend most of their time.'

"I used to see our women grow fed up with the world and all it contains and start complaining as soon as they're in their fifties, and I thought it was a woman's inevitable development until I met ... I forgot her name. Imagine!"

"That's all right. You've known her for over forty years."

"Let's call her Françoise."

"Is she French then?"

"I made a great effort to start that relationship. You've probably heard of the French seclusion. Well, in Françoise's case, it seemed rather to be self-consciousness with foreigners to the extent of shyness. So I persisted, because she was worth it. She was a retired history teacher and talking with her was always useful. We used to talk during and after lunch, which often lasted up to three hours. Then we parted in contentment."

"How was her husband?"

"Abominable. Not a word, not a smile, like the angel of death. He'd gulp down his food and sneak away."

"French arrogance, huh?"

"Laden with prejudice and that scornful toleration. Then, all of a sudden, their standard declined."

"How's that?"

"Well, there were no more flowers. The rugs and furniture were replaced by jute mats, reed bookcases and couches, and fine upholstery and curtains with rough Bedouin fabrics. They stopped eating in restaurants. She no longer asked me to lunch, and they seemed to begin a really hard life, but she still had her personal distinction and value."

"They must have been fearful of the future."

"I think so. That's why, when she invited me at Christmas, I told her that I'd take care of the dinner, because she likes my couscous, and that I had been missing it myself for a long time and it had to be shared. The kitchen and Christmas tree were sparkling, the former for lack of utilization and the latter with colors and lights but nothing else. And we spent the evening in a friendly and warm atmosphere.

"Then I received a money order from a woman I don't know. She called to say: 'I'm a friend of Françoise's husband. He tells me that he cannot get you out of his mind ... Hello! Are you there?' 'Yes.' 'He says that he's sending you five thousand dirhams through me and he asks you not to tell Françoise.' 'Sorry,' I burst out. 'I cannot. I'll send the money back to you. Return it to him.'"

"And then?"

"I returned the money and ended my relationship with Françoise, who must have said to her husband, shrugging in disdain: 'Those Arabs!' And you say now that disparities are a solution. Don't you see? Neither the religious disparities, nor the cultural ones, nor the difference in age, not even arrogance, could stop the guy from falling."

"You're using an interesting word, 'falling,' to describe the man's deed. The English say: 'to fall in love.' The French, '*tomber amoureux*.' We say: '*waqa'a filhub*.' That deed is associated with falling in every language. How interesting!"

"Even in the vernacular we say, '*tah ma'aha*.' Interesting indeed, that languages would define meanings with precisely the same expressions and words."

"…"

"Well, what shall I do, sir?"

"You say that you're sixty. Try to get involved with youngsters."

"I did. It looks like I have used exactly the solutions you're suggesting."

"You've tried that one too? What happened?"

"I haven't told you? I'm a teacher of French. When I retired, last year, I began giving private lessons. A young man came to me. He wanted to work on conversation and pronunciation. He was not serious, really. A child of one of those parvenus who consider their bourgeoisie identity incomplete unless they can twist their tongues with the accent of Paris. He didn't attend regularly in the beginning, and when I said to him: 'You're ready to pay for your lessons, but you're not ready to take them,' he answered: 'It is not my money.' Twenty-five years old and his father is still paying for his private lessons."

"One reason why students make it in some developed countries is that they pay for their education."

"That's why they don't go on strike. Have you ever heard of an American student, for instance, going on strike?"

"Of course not."

"That student was bright. He became fluent in both conversation and pronunciation in less than six months. He had become punctual to a point that surprised me, but also aroused my suspicion."

"Why?"

"He started arriving in advance and hanging about. He began dropping by, pretending that he wanted to borrow or return a book or pick up a notebook he had left behind. He also began calling me for some silly reason or other."

"You shouldn't have assumed that you knew the facts."

"I'm not a child, and I am able to know that state when I see it."

"Did you have other indications?"

"He started coming to class in his best attire, with polished shoes and that greasy stuff in his hair. And he became overcome by melancholy, thoughtfulness, and confusion. I thought of the only possible solution. I said I'll toss it out and see what happens. I told him in the middle of a lesson that Gérard Philipe would now envy his pronunciation, that I had nothing more to teach him, that he should forget the lessons and devote himself to his other occupations. I held my breath. His face muscles trembled, and he said: 'I swear to God, I will not forget.' And he burst into tears. So, I put away my reference books and programs and nipped all of those private lessons in the bud."

"It's a likely predicament. The student and the teacher, the patient and the physician."

"And what about Françoise's husband? Don't tell me the old man and the youth. There's always a justification, of course, but that's not what I'm asking about."

"Are you good-looking?"

"Me? I don't know. I haven't thought about it. I do hear it sometimes, and it always surprises me. Why this question?"

"Because a woman's good looks are a temptation calling for the veil, as a 'closure of the means.'"

"What's a closure of the means?"

"Prevention measures, in today's jargon, like preventing women from driving so they won't commit fornication."

"And then leave them in privacy with drivers. But scholars also say: 'A woman's virtue is her veil.' Besides, can beauty be hidden by a veil?"

"When it's flagrant, it calls for the face coverage too."

"I saw that in my mother's time, covering women with secrecy and magnifying their appeal. Besides, are good looks women's monopoly?"

"No man has ever come to me complaining about women's harassment and never will."

"Prophet Joseph did. Let me ask you. Had Prophet Joseph come to you, would you have suggested the veil? His good looks were a great temptation indeed."

"..."

"Well sir?"

"I don't know. The temptation may be your wit or perhaps your conduct towards others. I'm not sure of anything except for one. Your voice."

"What do you mean?"

"I want to see you. Your voice ..."

"You too? I cannot believe it. Farewell, sir."

The Baker

Hajj Madani's father came to Rabat around 1940 from the Draa Valley in the Sahara. Then, Ocean, Akkari, and Yacoub Al-Mansour neighborhoods in the city were still a wilderness.

In the Valley, Hajj Madani's father could do anything. He worked in construction, in road building, in agriculture. He served as water seller, and during the month of Ramadan it was he who woke people up for the last meal before dawn. He was often hired as a cook for weddings and what have you. "Seven skills and a meager livelihood," the proverb says. And Hajj Madani's father's livelihood stayed meager, even after he came to Rabat and joined his brother at the Jardins d'essais in the Avenue de la Victoire and was given the name of "the gardener." Thanks to his and his brother's hard work, those famous Experimental Gardens took shape and grew. He was proud of them then, at the time of the French when they were real gardens, but now....

Never mind. So, at any rate, Hajj Madani's father came to Rabat and built a cabin on the coast, next to his brother's, on open land that belonged to nobody. "Built" is not exactly the word because, as a matter of fact, the dwellings were made of sheets of old tin. Those two cabins were the first tin houses in the first shantytown in Rabat.

The two brothers would perform their dawn prayer, sling their lunch bags across their shoulders, and hit the hard ground to the gardens. They did not get home until the shadows of the landscape had stretched into a good length. When they married and brought their wives down from the valley, each one surrounded his yard with a fence of purple volubilis (oleander) flowers.

Word of the brothers went back home, and soon young men in the valley, when they reached adulthood, would put on their shoes and take off for Rabat. There, they joined the two brothers in their wilderness, registered to work at the gardens, and eventually built their own cabins of old tin sheets and fenced them with purple volubilis flowers.

In that wilderness, Hajj Madani was born. He was still a kid when the two tin cabins spread out and became a huge shantytown with mosques, bakeries, bath houses, infirmaries, schools, markets, and dishwashing water from undug sewers, where Hajj Madani often waded, barefoot, with children his own age. The shantytown people were like one family, same accent, same customs, same looks, everything. Had it not been for the tin and the ocean, one would think one was back in the Draa Valley.

When Hajj Madani was seven, his father took him to school one rainy morning. The father held his son's small hand in his iron fist and carried the boy's satchel. At the school gate, he knelt down, so that his wide, black face under a red Fez was at the same level with his son's. He placed the satchel handle in the boy's small grasp and covered it with his hands. "There, sonny!" he said. "Here're your books. Do your best, so you won't become a workingman, like your father. Go!" He stood up and, giving the child a pat on the back, added, "Study if you're gonna study." And Hajj Madani's father stood there staring at him and seeing nobody but him in the crowd of children, as the boy walked forward, stiff in his shoes and clothes from the feast before the last, clothes and shoes that had grown too tight.

When classes were over, the purple flowers and leaves outside the school were glistening in a soft light and the father was there waiting, holding a Moroccan doughnut in a palm leaf. He handed the doughnut to the boy and with the other hand touched his small head. Then father and son headed back home.

"Pa!" said the boy all of a sudden.

"Yes, sonny!"

"Someone stole my stuff."

The tough hand fell, like a hammer, on the back of the small head, and the doughnut flew up and landed in a pool of rainwater. The boy got home in tears. When his mother heard the news, she slapped her breast in consternation. His father swore that nothing was to be gained by this child's going to school. Then, grabbing his beard, he dared his wife to shave it if this child succeeded in school.

And so it was, as though the father had foretold the future, that Hajj Madani stayed ten years in primary school. He would study a book two years in a row and wear it out without understanding a thing in it. How many times did his mother take him to Qur'an reciters, fortunetellers and shrines! How much incense did not she burn for him! How many magic herb infusions did she not make him gulp! How many charms did she not make him wear! Hajj Madani felt he had gone through hell before he finally learned the good news of his expulsion.

The director summoned his father and said, "This child has been ten years at this school. But he has learned nothing. We don't grant graduation by seniority, you know." So the iron hand fell once more on the back of the small head.

At home the mother, who had heard the bad news, slapped her breast again, and the neighbors came to offer their sympathy:

"It's God's will."

"God chooses what's best."

"Being expelled from school never killed anyone."

"Send him to learn a trade. God will provide for him."

Thus Hajj Madani became a baker's apprentice. He woke up with the rooster, opened the bakery, removed the ashes, and cleaned the oven room. Then, he brought in the wood, lit a new fire, and started to align the dough boards. When the dough was brought to the oven, he stacked the boards carefully. He picked up the baked round loaves as they came out of the oven and placed each back on the board it had come on. He placed the boards on shelves and then returned them to their owners in a clock-like precision. During rush hours, he practically flew from one board to another.

In the afternoons, he cut the firewood. Well, it was what the boss called "firewood," chunks of tree-roots, which looked like huge molar teeth. The roots were as hard as rock, and the axe got stuck in them. At the end of the first days, Hajj Madani would go back home with skinned palms. But in the course of time, the root began to split easily for him, as easily as if it were a watermelon. Hajj Madani's talents developed so much in harmony with his trade that he turned to it with all his heart, especially on Thursdays when he got his pay and gave it to his father.

Within three years time, he became a master baker, jumping proudly down into the hole to be at level with the oven, as if he were a fierce Al-hilali hero. He would halt briefly between batches to gulp a puff of hashish and a draught of strong tea.

Since his weaning, his mother had worked in the mornings as a maid for a French family and woven rugs for the rest of the day. She put all her money in a piece of cloth, tied it firmly, inserted it inside her mattress, and slept on it.

In the Year of Independence, the year Hajj Madani became a baker, the French family went back to their homeland, leaving their furnished villa to his mother in exchange for her savings from housework and weaving. Thus, by an extraordinary stroke of good luck, Hajj Madani's family began to live in the most chic neighborhood of Rabat.

The land of the old tin cabin was sold for a handsome sum, since the shantytown had become part of the city, and the price of a square meter there had gone up. As for the shack itself and the volubilis flowers, a tractor swept them away in less than no time.

Some days later, the family sat down to discuss the villa.

"We'll live on the first floor," said the mother "and Madani (he did not yet have his title of Hajj because he had not performed the pilgrimage to Mecca yet) can turn the ground floor into a bakery."

Father and son agreed, especially since the neighborhood was getting Moroccanized after the departure of the French. And that is how Hajj Madani became the first baker in Agdal, the fashionable quarter of Rabat. His bakery had been functioning years before any one had heard of the mosque or the bathhouse in that neighborhood.

The family stayed unchanged. It did not turn its back on the shantytown or look down on the people who still lived there. It behaved as if it had not become a villa dweller. Therefore, Hajj Madani's bride came right from that shantytown.

When his parents passed away, Hajj Madani's attitude toward the shantytown people remained the same. His business prospered so much that the bakery began to stay open day and night, for he had signed contracts with caterers. He performed the big pilgrimage to Mecca seven times, and also the small one. Now, he sits formally behind a wooden counter with two framed inscriptions hanging above him. One displays the Purity Surat[1] from the Qur'an, and the other reports the charge for bread and cookies. During rush hours, when he sees his bakery working full speed and coins pouring into his moneybox, he thinks of school and thanks God that he was expelled.

---

[1] Purity, Qur'an. Chapter CXII. Say thou (Mohamed): He is Allah, the One. Allah, the Independent. He begets not, nor was He begotten. And never there has been anyone co-equal with Him.

Two Stories of a House

"Khadija Bent Ahmed! Meeluda Bent Al-bacheer!"

At this resounding call, two old women in the waiting room gathered up the voluminous folds of their veils with their designs of blooming red roses. They rushed to the courtroom and stood in front of the judge. He was turning over some papers on his desk.

"Khadija Bent Ahmed!"

"Yes sir!"

"Did you leave your house of your own free will?"

"I didn't sir! This Meeluda told me I could come back. She swore by Mecca that I could come back as soon as her ceiling was repaired. Her ceiling is the floor of my house, sir. So I left everything there. I only took my clothes, because she said the repairs would just take a month. But she broke the landing and demolished the stairs. Now, my two rooms are like they are suspended in the air. I can't get to them, sir. It has been two years. And because my rooms are suspended, I go to my brother's for a while and then to my sister's. It's just two rooms, true, but it's my little home."

She burst into tears, wiped her eyes with the hem of her veil, and began to sob like a child. "I entered that house as a bride," she went on, "and I intended to stay there till the end of my days. Haven't we paid for it? Yes we have, more than its worth, in the thirty years we have been living there."

"Big deal," snorted the defendant. "Forty dirhams a month. What's that? It wouldn't buy even a kilogram of meat."

"Stop it!" shouted Khadija. "What about the blood? Your blood from childbirth that I cleaned with my own hands? What about the meals I cooked for your feasts and your mourning ceremonies? What about your children, who grew up on my back? It's thirty years, six hundred and sixty monthly rents, two million centimes, perhaps more. Couldn't that amount have bought us your house and mine? Couldn't it? If it weren't for my late husband's carelessness and extravagance. They call it generosity! He wasted his money feeding his ungrateful, so-called friends. Meat was brought to our house seven kilos at a time. If he ..."

"Forget your late husband now, will you?" ordered the judge. "Was it your husband who told you to lock the house and give the key to the defendant?"

"I didn't give her the key, sir. The key is still with me." She raised her skirts, bent over, and pulled from the pocket of her bloomers a big black key. "There! But what good is it? The house has no stairs and no landing. It's suspended in the air."

"You mean you just locked the door and walked away?"

"Well, she's my neighbor and she swore by Mecca. Wouldn't a good Muslim lock the door and walk away? I believed her."

"What do you want now?"

"My home!" Tears overwhelmed her again and she murmured as if to herself: "I can't stop crying when I pronounce that word." And to the judge: "I am frightened of moving, very anxious, as if I was being expatriated or was dying. It's my little home, sir." She started to cry again.

"Where have you been all this time? Why haven't you submitted your case to the court before?"

"I had it in the hands of saints, sir."

"And you took it back, I guess," said the judge, smiling. The audience smiled, too. Then he asked the defendant: "What's your statement?"

"Two years ago, bless you, sir, dirt started coming down from my ceiling. So, I asked this person to evacuate her house above it, so we could repair the ceiling. But when the worker touched it, the landing collapsed, and carried the staircase with it. Were it not for God's grace, the poor man could have lost his life. That's the whole story."

"What are you saying?" cried Khadija. "You swore by Mecca, Meeluda! You said to leave for a month! You said you'd do the repairs and I could come back!"

"Stop wailing! There's no way to fix it. The whole house is collapsing, for heaven's sake!"

"Enough!" ordered the judge, then pronounced the following sentence: "Tomorrow morning, if God wills it, at ten sharp local firemen will bring Khadija Bent Ahmed's belongings from the house located in number 3 Baker Street. She will take her possessions, in the presence of the police, and return the key to its proprietor. Case closed. Next."

That day Khadija Bent Ahmed learned that a divorced old woman was renting a room in the house she had once lived in.

The old woman now lived in a wooden hut on the roof. On the ground floor, an old man occupied another room with his wife, a rough country girl hardly twenty years old, baked by the sun from work in the fields.

Khadija Bent Ahmed told her story to the old woman on the roof.

"Oh! my neigh... I was going to say my neighbor. Excuse me, but I called someone by that name and I am a dummy to honor her so."

"Tell me about it," said the old lady. "There's no good neighbor in this world, no grateful people, no faithful husbands. You say that Meeluda was your neighbor for thirty years and threw you out. Well, my story is worse." She gestured to the ground floor with one earring, "I've been married to the old man down there for forty years, but after he saw that country bumpkin he ignored me completely."

"And who sent him the country bumpkin?"

"I did. I brought her to him myself. I found her shedding tears in the shrine. She was pregnant. She was scared of her brothers and was hiding there. So I said to myself: 'Well, there's an unborn she's carrying with terror while you have no children at all. Why don't you take her home and when she delivers, she'll go away and you will have the baby.'

"That slut said to me: 'This shrine is a witness between you and me.' And we concluded a pact on the saint's tomb, according to which I would hide her shame and she would leave me the baby. She stayed with me till she gave birth, with God's omnipotence, to twin boys. The old man registered them in our family booklet at once.

"I took care of her as if she were my own child. It was out of the question to let her go right after she gave birth. I said to myself: 'Wait one week,' and at the end of the week I said: 'Wait another week!' Then the old man said: 'You've accomplished a good deed, carry it to the end. Keep her a bit longer. She'll breast feed the babies and she'll finish her forty days. God will reward you.' 'Amen!' said I."

"And at the end of the forty days," said Khadija Bent Ahmed in a teasing tone, "you said you'd keep her until the babies were weaned?"

"No. At the end of the forty days, I took her to the public bath, dyed her hands and feet with henna, gave her some money and presents, and said to her: 'It's time for you to go.' 'Oh no,' she retorted. 'It's rather time for you to go. I'm here in my own house, with my children.' And she pulled out a marriage contract."

"The old man married her?"

"And repudiated me."

"What a fool! But it's your fault. You let her stay. She's breast fed her children and gotten attached to them."

"Well, when she waved that marriage contract at me, I ran to my chest, got out my family booklet, and shoved it in her face, saying: 'You can have the old man but you will never have the babies.' I slipped the booklet in my shirt, took the twins in my arms, rushed up to my hut and locked it."

"But why do you stay in the same house?"

"Where would I go? I have no family, and the life savings I earned with my sweat are in that house. You say that Meeluda swore by Mecca? Well my country bumpkin concluded a pact with me on the saint's tomb."

The twins are three years old now. When the old woman goes out, she slides a sheet of tin over the grillwork that covers the patio opening and then she locks the roof door. As soon as she has gone, the country girl takes a long reed pole and pushes the tin sheet away with it. She calls out: "Hassan! Hussein!" And when the boys' faces show up at the opening, she stretches the reed out to them and there are sweets tied at the end of it.

A Notion of Progress

"Do you think Morocco has progressed?" Catherine asked me, as we stepped out of my neighborhood post office.

"Yes. Of course," I replied without thinking.

"How?"

"In comparison with other countries in the continent."

"In what way?"

"Infrastructure, human resources.... Do you know that there is a Central African country that has no more than two hundred kilometers of paved roads, and one North African country has no drainage system. Infrastructure is the sign of real progress, not abortion rights."

"For me, computers are the sign. When I came to Morocco ten years ago, I did not see a single computer, but yesterday when I was coming back from Marrakech, for the first time I saw a man on the train working with a portable computer on his knees. One of those guys who wear corduroy trousers and monogrammed shirts. I wanted to talk to him, but I was afraid he might think I was trying to seduce him."

"That's what he would have thought, but the notion of progress is relative. Some will tell you: 'When artists can survive on their art, that's where progress lies.' Computers are important, of course, and cyber cafés are popping up in cities and villages like mushrooms in autumn. But education is more important. Unfortunately, illiteracy is still overwhelming."

"Teaching grownups is not easy. I agree."

"If only we had focused on teaching children."

"What do you make of the slogan, 'education is free and compulsory'?" She said disapprovingly, raising her eyebrows in disbelief.

"It's a formula. But if someone decided not to send their children to school, nobody would force them to do it. Come on, Catherine, if they wanted to erase illiteracy, they'd have made education really compulsory."

She tossed her head defiantly and continued: "Why did you say that Morocco is progressing then?"

"I said in comparison with the past and with similar countries. Anyway, it's like the half-filled glass; it depends on which half you want to look at. Like calling Morocco Islamic. Yes, mosques are packed, but so are bars."

"It's a developing country, to use some of the jargon."

"Exactly. Take the post office, for instance; you should have seen how it was a decade ago. I used to feel anxious whenever I walked up to it, like a child on his way to be vaccinated."

On that note, I left Catherine and went on my way with our conversation still in my head. Suddenly, the word "vaccination" formed itself in my mind. I remembered having written it some time ago in my own notes about that very post office. When I got home, I went right to my old notebooks and began leafing through them. An idea occurred to me. I thought that those who write journals will have themselves as readers in the future and that a writer has to have a reader or he will not exist.

In those notes I found ideas, expressions, words I had cherished as if they were texts of special quality. And they were of value, since I could judge them now with greater neutrality, because I have been separated from them for so many years. I have kept such notes since I was in the fourth grade. Others collect stamps, but I collect words. I select them with care, put them down in a dignified hand, and handle them with delight like diamonds.

Engrossed, I spent three full hours reading my old notes until I came upon the piece I had been looking for, which I reproduce here in its entirety:

"As I walked to the post office this morning, I had the same feeling that seizes children on their way to vaccination. My neighborhood post office is as large as a classroom. It has three windows and a counter from the days of colonization, when it was built to serve only a few thousand settlers. Now, a mass of human beings is crammed into its narrow space. This is not because the people don't understand the concept of order, but because the place is so small there is not room for a straight line to form. Also, the woman employee is extremely slow.

"Last month, a man I know was standing in the back of the line. He announced he was unable to wait any more, that he had left his office and couldn't linger any longer. A young French man, also in the back, said to his friend, in a colonialist tone, that he did not understand all this waste of time to pay a damn phone bill, that all he had to do in France was put a check in the mail. 'C'est une poste café,' he or his friend remarked, and I understood that you come to that poste café to stay. According to a Moroccan saying, 'Going out of the bath house is not like coming in.'

"The man I know was now in front, telling those protesting that he was not the only one who had tried to jump the queue. Still, it was not long before he decided to sneak away. This month I delayed my phone bill payment till the deadline, but things in the post office were just the same. People were fidgety, some were mumbling. One person asked, 'Is this post office going to be like this forever?' No one answered. The woman employee continued writing slowly. I stayed in that crooked line thirty-five minutes, until five p.m. And I was lucky, because some swore that they had been there since two-thirty. They told about a fight between the employee and a woman who wanted to pay for a letter with a big banknote after she had already stuck on the stamp. They said that a colleague of the employee called the woman by an obscene name and that the employee, after the woman left, took her letter out of the mailbox.

"In this case, the balance of power shifted back and forth between the employee and the people. The atmosphere changed from understanding and endurance to protest and anger. One man, probably new to this post office, said with a kind of tolerance that the place was small and disproportionate to the number of people in the neighborhood.

"Half an hour later, the employee began telling people to form a straight line and let air come in. But given the long time they had been there, no one could remember who was in front of whom. They became confused and began saying things like they had been here since two-thirty and what line was she talking about. They said that there were two lines at the beginning, but the employee said she did not give a damn. A man tried to give her some advice, but she replied: 'Come work in my place and see what it is like.'

"At that point, I was amazed by the magnitude of this waste of time. The group became two lines again, and the employee continued her deliberate writing, and the man who was saying that people do not know order said that she was slow. 'Ce n'est pas le Cap Canavéral,' he said aloud, meaning the Kennedy Center for Space Research. He then asked why the woman had to perform the tasks, '*Mais qu'est-ce qu'elle fait? Pourquoi ne nous laisse-t-elle pas remplir nos reçus nous-mêmes?*'

"'She writes the date,' a man in khaki answered him in Arabic, 'and the amount of postage, sticks on the stamp, and then impresses her official stamp.' The first man said that he could do that himself and suggested that the post office does not trust technology. It has developed the telephone, but not human resources. Everything is still done manually.

"'Banks are in better shape,' someone in the front commented. 'They, at least, combine manual and technical skills.' And the first man replied again in French that the telephone is part of business, and the post office supervisor should have supplied two employees. Then, shifting to Arabic, he said, 'We want to give them money but they won't take it.'"

October 12, 1989.

I put down the notebook, saying with a giggle: "There's your proof, Catherine, if only you could read Arabic."

The Ranch

He was a police commissioner in Casablanca before becoming the manager of factories that produced jeans and alcohol. From his former role, he had learned how to spur on his workers. He was a devil of a man, skinny, tall, with a slightly bent back, a bony face, a long sharp nose, and a few hairs puffed up on his skull.

How does a police commissioner turn into a manager of two factories? This was a question his workers asked each other, looking right and left before they spoke, for the man was dangerous. They were careful, since those were the days when one had difficulty getting a job to provide for one's family's basic needs.

Nevertheless, there was not a soul in either factory who did not know about the ranch on the road to the airport and its sumptuous mansion. The place was a farm, actually. People call it a ranch, ironically, after the *Dallas* TV serial.

When a person pressed the gate bell at the ranch, a voice answered on an internal phone, inquiring about the visitor's identity and the nature of his visit. Then, just like Ali Baba's grotto, the gate opened all by itself, so they say. Exactly as in the fairy tale. A girl would appear in a sort of air-hostess uniform and lead one in, holding herself erect on her pointed high heels. One walked along a path through abundant greenery and colorful blossoms, through a blend of fragrances, and past water fountains gushing out and flowing into marble basins.

Indoors, one's breath was taken away by the splendor of the interior. Qur'anic verses in fine calligraphy carved on marble and in dark and light brown cedar wood, arabesques, *mashrabiah* screens, silk rugs, objects of art.... By night, lamps concealed atop the high walls shed indirect illumination on the ceilings, giving an impression of daylight. From outdoors, the mansion in the dusk looks like a diamond, sparkling upon the black velvet of the night. A fabulous place!

The ranch cost hundreds of millions. Imagine! Easy to say, but if one were to pick up one million pebbles in the river, one could not pick up enough. They said that the cost included other structures such as the swimming pool, the tennis court, the stables, the birds in huge cages, the fish in ponds, the fountains, and the gardens....

The manager spent lavishly on that ranch from his wine business, because he said he wanted to put the dirty money in dirt and walls. As for the clean business, the one making jeans, he put that in a separate bank account from which he paid for his and his wife's annual pilgrimages to Mecca during the last ten days of Ramadan. This custom provided another opportunity for people to whisper:

"That fellow is playing with money."

"Diseased money. May God guard us from it."

"Why doesn't he content himself with the religiously permissible money, the money from the jeans factory?"

"It does not make as much profit."

"And he dares make the pilgrimage to Mecca!"

"He reminds me of a girl I know. She goes to clubs, dances, and drinks, all that stuff. Then she does not go to bed until she's performed her dawn prayer. I swear to God."

"Happy new world."

Then poof, incredible news came that the man had been arrested for selling outdated beer. The whispers were back:

"They call him to account for selling outdated beer, but why do they let him sell beer at all in a Muslim country?"

"The virus of doing the wrong thing is getting to him, then."

When the man went to jail, his henchmen began bragging about the comforts of his cell, its fancy furniture, electronic appliances, air conditioner, mini bar, gourmet food, and visitors. At last, the man could relax, he who never had a break except for Ramadan pilgrimages of course.

The whispers:

"A five-star cell."

"Nonsense. A bond is a bond were it made of silk."

"Prison is recreation now, it seems."

"Well, they're in it. They've got to make it comfy."

"Goddamn! Shameless, that's what they are."

So, the man stayed in that cell for a while, then was released in obscure circumstances. The minute he was free, he began implementing a plan to promote what he called his spiritual beverages. Within a year, the business doubled. So, whispers were back:

"My goodness! Looks like he planned it in jail."

"Surely it is not the eyes that are blinded, but blinded are the hearts that are in the breasts."[1]

"Jail didn't shake his belief in that alcohol, then."

"He took a liking to the gains of it."

"Why shouldn't he? Is there something that bans it or someone to say: 'Fear God'?"

"Who can say it? Don't you see how people shrink in front of that man, bad as he is?"

"The next blow will finish him, I'm telling you."

That year, when he and his wife came back from their Ramadan pilgrimage, they found the ranch in a dreadful condition. May God protect us. A stinking smell filled the air. Black plastic bags were caught in the trees and flowers and in the wires of the bird cages. They were scattered about the lawn, swooping up to the sky with bits of plastic smoke.

Indoors, smoke hung from the ceilings and in the corners, stuck to the upholstery, the curtains, the engravings, and rested on the rugs.

> *Wherefore there visited an incircling visitation while they slept.*
>
> *Then in the morning it became as if it had been plucked.*[2]

The wife fainted before she heard the guard explaining the catastrophe. "The lands all around have been established as a dump site for Casablanca, sir. I'm sorry. But don't be upset. It's only dirt and walls, as you often said."

And so saying, the guard thought to himself: "And why should you get upset? It's easy come, easy go, as they say, or in this case, ill-gotten, easy go."

---

[1] Qur'an. Al-Haj (Pilgrimage). Verse 46.

[2] Qur'an. Al-Qalam (The Pen). Verses 19 & 20.

What Attitude?

This morning, there are two chairs at the entrance of my apartment building. One is a cane chair, worn at the bottom and covered with a dark and soft piece of linen. This is Mohamed's chair. He lives down the hall with his wife and three children. His chair was already there when I moved into the building some three years ago. The other chair is made of metal and has a red leather seat. It belongs to a new watchman, whose name nobody knows except the tenant in apartment number 18.

So now our building has two watchmen, and there is a reason for this. The tenant in apartment 18 wrote a letter in poor Arabic, which he slipped under all our doors. In that letter, he claimed that Mohamed did not do his work, and that someone had attacked his wife (number 18's wife) in the lift with a pocketknife, the very day he wrote, at four-fifteen p.m.

He summoned the police, who knocked on Mohamed's door. Mohamed came out wiping his eyes. Every time someone knocks on his door, he comes out wiping his eyes. The man sleeps instead of watching the building. Since he is paid to watch, not sleep, he should be fired. Meanwhile, number 18 has hired a new watchman at his own expense.

That's what the letter says. In the lobby, however, the tenant of apartment 18 tells everybody who will listen that Mohamed is an informer and the police wouldn't be tough with him, even if fifteen cops had showed up the day of the attack. Number 18 had said to them: "Take him!" but they answered that there was nothing in the law allowing them to take him. He then announced that he would call the Minister of Home Affairs himself.

Mohamed denies the allegation completely. He says in his strong Berber accent that number 18 is trying to get hold of his room, to store his boxes in it, boxes loaded with God knows what. God also knows where they come from. They are so heavy that one man cannot move them by himself. They must be filled with lead or something, Mohamed adds.

Mohamed went to see the man who last year opened a coffee shop on the ground floor of our apartment building without the permission of the inhabitants. He said to him:

"Have you ever heard of anybody who was attacked and there was no injury or blood or witnesses?"

"Number 18 is just lying, you mean."

"Well, he wants my room to stock his boxes in it, that's all."

"Well," said the coffee shop owner, "You just wait and see." To Mohamed's stupefaction, the man explained that he wanted to take that room, that he would turn it into a kitchen for his coffee shop.

This year, the new watchman graduated from Law School. He wears jeans, American T-shirts, and sports shoes. He sits on his chair on the right side of the entrance, seemingly despondent. When the sun reaches him, he moves to the opposite side of the street and watches the building from there, through his gold-rimmed sunglasses. As for Mohamed's chair, it still sits in the landing, unoccupied most of the time.

Every time I pass by the new watchman, he looks down. Does he think that I am accusing him of trying to take the means of subsistence away from Mohamed, a poor man, the father of a family?

One morning I said to him: "*Assalamu 'alaykum!*" as I passed. He raised his head and returned my salutation cheerfully. From then on, every time I greeted him and he returned it with a pleasant smile, I thought of another face from twelve years ago.

I had been living for six months in Austin, Texas, in a private students' residence. I wanted to adjust a little before daring to live by myself. My mates were wealthy Texas students. They had arrived with their luxurious furniture, carpets, paintings, stereos, phones, cars, and also their caste spirit, which stupefied me. I had come there thinking that Texans were mere cowboys. But their attitude did not bother me, because I had decided to move anyway.

A Moroccan girl I had met at the mosque invited me to share her flat. Every Friday after prayers, she would tell me again that her apartment was spacious and furnished with what her Muslim sisters had left her when they finished their studies and departed. All I'd have to do was to share the rent and bills. I accepted finally because of her insistence on the one hand, and on the other because she seemed reliable. Did not she wear a veil, even if it was sometimes transparent? Besides, sharing her flat would decrease my expenses and hers, and I would be spared the trouble of looking for a place by myself.

At the end of the term, the residents left. Recent graduates had hired moving vans, which they loaded with all their belongings and drove off in a din of country music. Nobody was left in the residence but me. I packed my possessions in two suitcases and my books in a box, and I called the Moroccan sister:

"*Assalamu 'alaykum!*"

"*Wa 'alaykumu assalam!*"

"Are you home? Can I come along?"

"Yes, but I must tell you something," she said. "I have all this furniture here, which will save you a lot of expenses. So you must pay the rent and bills entirely, because I'm providing the furniture."

"Thank you! *Assalamu 'alaykum!*"

I had only three hours before the residence closed. I called a real estate agent at once. Five minutes later, I was in one of the agent's cars. He was explaining that the apartments in the complex we were going to visit in the south of the city were equipped only with refrigerators and cooking stoves.

Half an hour later, I was back at the students' residence office concluding another deal, according to which the residence kept my advance and I took my room furniture in return. When I asked the director for suggestions about how to move it, he said that the Mexican man who worked in the kitchen had a pick-up and might want the work of transporting my furniture.

Another half hour later, the Mexican had put everything in its place in my new apartment. I was thanking him at the front door and opening my purse, but he said firmly: "I'm not taking a cent from you. I decided it the minute I saw you at the director's office. If it was one of those Americans, I would never have agreed to do this move, even if they gave me a hundred dollars. But you, because of your attitude towards us, I will not take a cent from you. Why, when you pass me your tray through the kitchen window after you have finished your meal, you don't have that attitude!"

Now, in Rabat, every time I see the new watchman raise his head and cheerily return my greeting, I think of that Mexican man, and I wonder what attitude he was talking about.

From the Diary of a
Parliamentary Employee

Monday. My first day in the parliament. When the administrative director introduced me to the vice president, the man became very angry. "Now you find a position, but when I wanted to hire my people, you said: 'There are no positions.' Three of the president's chronies have been employed, so three of my people should also be hired. Or else."

The administrative director's countenance turned to resentment and mine to stupor. It was like I was in the market place rather than the House of Parliament. When we walked out, the administrative director muttered a dirty insult: "Those guys fight for positions and trips," he said. "They boast about luxury sedans imported duty free. Right in the chamber they talk about 'the right man in the right place,' 'saving,' and of course 'modernity' and 'democracy.' Goddamn!"

What a disappointment! But what can you do?

Tuesday. There are no women in this parliament except for the secretaries. So, I share my office with a male colleague. At nine o'clock, an employee named Saida came to him with her usual load of gossip: "The one you know, she's making a fortune from land parcels she buys for next to nothing, from office boys who beg them in the halls, from every new minister of housing. And that other one, she rents a furnished flat per night to some representatives for an outrageous sum of money in exchange for having a place for the debauchery that goes on around here. At least they get their piece of the pie. Not like us."

She walked to the window and flung it open. A cold wind came in and my nose began running at once. What a place for me to be!

Wednesday. My cold is getting worse. I cannot decide whether to keep my sweater on or take it off. When Saida showed up, she started right away: "The one who went to a conference in Moscow, he gave them a hard time when they tried to put him in a tourist class, then he spent the entire time drinking, from the moment he settled in his first class seat to the moment he landed back in Casablanca. This is the man who shouts in the chamber, 'Praise be to God. May prayer and peace be upon the Messenger of God.' 'Our true religion,' 'Our Islamic reference,' and of course 'Modernity' and 'Democracy.'"

I cannot find a comfortable position. Saida opened the window for the wind to strike me.

Friday. I got a flu vaccine at the parliament infirmary, and off I went to one of the meetings I had been attending with members of several government ministries, at a women's association. It was all about a proposal to revise family law. And, because the association had only typewriters, I volunteered to enter the proposal into my office computer.

Monday. The vaccine had no effect. I was simply falling down on my feet. Doctors had no idea what might have caused this flu. Finally, I went to a specialist. "Pollution." he said, "The culprit is water. Don't let water into your nose. That's all."

"Yes but how about my ablutions and cleaning myself for my prayer?" I asked, very annoyed.

"God's religion is wide," he replied in a reproachful tone. "There's *tayammum*, or do you think you're a better Muslim than the great mosque's imam? Well, he's using tayammum, you know."

I could kill Saida. Damn her for opening that window.

Tuesday. Thank God, I finished entering the proposal into the computer. I went to work earlier than usual, in that elation that comes with achievement. I turned the computer on, eager to print the draft at last, but the file was gone. In plain English, stolen. What? Who? Why? After all, it was in the computer, which was in a locked office. The key was with security in the parliament compound. What will I say when I go to the meeting tomorrow?

Thursday. I went to the meeting somewhat at a loss. But the representative of the Ministry of Home Affairs spared me an explanation. She is a short, stout woman. Her face has been darkened by the sun. Her country countenance has not been altered with the acquisition of her fortuitous wealth. Like Moroccan officers in the old colonial army, she speaks French, twisting her mouth as she does so. Then she would lift her chest and tilt her nose as she walked in her somber, tight suits, her hands extended behind her, her shoulders swaying back and forth.

She took out a bundle of papers as soon as she came in and began distributing them, casting mean looks in my direction all the time. And what do you think the handouts were? The stolen file, now in laser print on sumptuous paper, bearing the letterhead of the Ministry of Home Affairs.

"That's it now," she said, dusting off her hands and striding to her seat where she began jabbering, "*Il faut bien cibler si nous voulons que la femme obtienne ses droits dans le Maroc de la modernité et de la démocratie.*" (We have to aim our target carefully if we want women to obtain their rights in a Morocco of modernity and democracy.)

Monday. I began leafing through the papers. Nothing in them except for the news of thirty-five women entering the parliament under a policy set up by the government. Saida came in at her usual time: "You see that guy? He picked his wife. That other one chose his sister. The first one's wife pleaded for her sister, and he chose her too. Imagine! They lucked into a treasure. Millions will pour on them as they sleep. Millions they'd have never dreamed of had they spent their lives toiling as employees. Let alone when they pass the bill to increase Parliament salaries."

That tayammum bothers me, but what can I do?

A Paying Guest

When I went to work for the Moroccan Office for Commerce and Export in London, an English secretary there told me that finding accommodations would take some time and I could use her guest room in the meantime. I found her offer hard to believe, because of what I had heard about European sense of privacy, individualism, greed, and especially English indifference.

I was amazed by the hold that stereotypes could have. They were so strong that a story was still ringing in my ears, about a Moroccan fellow who, while visiting his daughter and her French husband in Paris, heard them fighting over a missing yogurt in the refrigerator, which he had helped himself to.

I said to myself, now: "One rotten fish makes the whole donkey bag smell," as Moroccans put it. "There she is, pure English! If helping me find accommodations is part of her job, where is her obligation to offer me her guest room?"

We spent the day looking into places, and, when we finally got to her house, she said: "We had a party here last night and there's some leftovers." And she handed me a toasted cheese sandwich and a nice "cuppa" tea, as they call it. Then, she ushered me to a splendid room upstairs, which smelled of newness, with a lovely pink carpet, white lace curtains, a quilt with a crimson print and matching ostrich-feather pillows, a fine chest of drawers with a huge china bowl on it, two sumptuous lamps on bed tables, rattan armchairs, a private bathroom with a high quality of ceramics and taps, big palm-leaf baskets with lids, soft crimson towels stacked on glass shelves, colored liquids in wonderful bottles, even a tooth brush in a sealed box, and fresh plants in porcelain pots. I was delighted and amazed by such a standard of generosity. Who would now dare say that Hatim (the Arab symbol of generosity) is no European?

The next morning, we had breakfast in the kitchen overlooking luxuriant herb and vegetable beds in the back garden. A variety of flowers stood in pots on the windowsill.

On the third day, we finally found a convenient place for me to live. Before taking leave, she handed me a folded piece of paper, which read as follows:

(Her full name and address at the top)

Invoice

London, May 3rd, 1968

To: (*My full name*)

DESCRIPTION	#	DATE	PRICE
Sandwich	1	1.5.1968	1 £
Cup of tea	1	" "	1 £
Bed	1	" "	30 £
Breakfast	1	2.5.1968	5 £
Bed	1	" "	30 £
Breakfast	1	3.5.1968	+5 £
Total			**72 £**

Seventy-two sterling pounds

The total was followed by her stamp and signature.

And then she took to reminding me whenever she had a chance about the time when I was her guest. She would say, "I want to change the curtains in my living room. The ones I had when you were my guest." Or, "The willow is casting its shadow on all of the second floor. I'm thinking of cutting it down. You probably remember it from when you were my guest."

"I was a paying guest," I finally stated one day, when I could take it no more. And that settled it, for she never went back to reminding me of when I was her guest.

Mrs. O'Grady

She worked at the Moroccan Tourist Office in London. She received visitors and provided them with leaflets, maps, and information. Whenever I came across her stiff, expressionless face and heard her harshly answering visitors' questions, I wondered where she came from. Some military barrack, perhaps.

She avoided the Moroccans in London but associated with their Jewish counterparts. She did not like Arabs, not even her colleagues, whom she treated with contempt. Her manners were French in character, and she spoke English with a French accent. Her French was provincial. She appeared to know some Arabic but used it reluctantly. Her knowledge of Morocco was merely functional.

From all this, I deduced that she must be a descendent of the French settlers who had seized, during colonization, Moroccan peasants' lands, and grown quite angry with Morocco when they were forced to return the lands after independence. My curiosity would have ended there, had I not discovered our protagonist's name. She was called Fatima El-Alawi. She was Moroccan, then!

There was in that Tourist Office another Arab girl who was from Palestine. Our Arabness had bound us with a sort of kinship. Some English people asked me about it, but I could not answer them, because there was nothing to compare it with. Not the Anglican Church, not the Anglo-Saxon culture, not even the commonwealth. I used to brush the question aside, well aware that Arabness escapes English people's comprehension, and that they will never understand why Palestine is a problem that involves all Arabs.

Every now and then, I picked up my friend at the office, and off we went for lunch in some restaurant or other in the Regent Street area. It was during one of these lunches that I asked her about her Moroccan colleague and learned that Fatima's father was a wealthy man from Casablanca and her mother the daughter of French farmers.

"Fatima is strange," said my friend.

"There are thousands like her."

"Why?"

"A huge number of Moroccans live in France, you know."

"Do they come back home with French wives?"

"Educated ones do. Workers come back with hard currency and look for a wife in some remote Moroccan village."

"I can't believe that a person would live in her country without speaking her language or participating in her own culture."

"That's because she lives in a closed circle," I retorted. "What I don't understand is how a French woman could marry a Moroccan man and spend the rest of her life in Morocco and never learn a word of Arabic, whereas any Moroccan worker who lands in Paris starts stammering French before the year is over."

"Colonialist mentality. It'll pass."

"What will stay," I commented, "is that Fatima's father has given his country a citizen who resents it."

"Yes, but the mother's influence outweighed his. Her relation with her daughter is one of flesh and blood. Yet the father is firmly attached to his Islamic convictions."

"How so?"

"Well," continued my friend, "he refuses to let Fatima marry her English Protestant boy friend. He threatened to cut her off completely if she does marry him."

"What does the rest of the family think?"

"She has only her mother in Casablanca and a brother in France, and they both support her against her father."

Another time, as I was picking up my friend for lunch, I heard someone calling for a Mrs. O'Grady. And who was Mrs. O'Grady but Fatima El-Alawi.

Medi

Othman was the first Moroccan to marry a French woman. He met Thérèse at his work place and fell in love with her fair hair and slim figure. He was also the first Moroccan to be employed, under French rule, by the Public Library in Fez and hence, the first Moroccan to discover the attraction of French living: how one's faculties are coaxed into harmony by refined cuisine, comfortable furniture, sumptuous curtains, subdued lights, soft music, and pleasant conversation, as well as flowers and perfume.

He sat in his new living room and felt that he was sitting in heaven. He thanked God for all his wellbeing and asked Him to make it last for ever. He never thought of trying to convert Thérèse to Islam, for the simple reason that she too was immersed in her religion, Christianity. He saw no harm in that, since her devotion made her a religious rather than a loose woman. On her part, Thérèse said to herself that actually they worshiped the same God, each in their own traditions.

During the first year of their marriage, they were extremely happy. At the beginning of the second, Thérèse gave birth to a boy. Othman walked into her room in the clinic and went straight to the little bed with its profusion of white and lace. He bent over, admiring the tiny fists, the closed eyes, and the dark hair brushed into a little crest. "You have your father's hair, Mohamed!" he exclaimed merrily.

"His name is Nicolas!" said Thérèse harshly. "There'll be no Mohamed, never!"

"There'll be no Nicolas," retorted Othman, his mirth draining away, "never!"

For a whole month the baby stayed without a name. And over the house hung a sullenness, a dry animosity, to such an extent that when Othman sat in the living room, he felt he was sitting in hell. One day some good friends suggested giving the baby a neutral name. They proposed a list and the couple chose Mahdi. But from the very first day, the name became Médi in the mouth of the mother and her circle. Later, the distortion was confirmed at the French school the boy attended, and also in his own mouth because he could not speak Arabic and thus could not even pronounce his name properly.

107

Thérèse, who had learned her lesson, employed methods at her disposal to prevent a second pregnancy, and Othman implicitly approved. Thus Médi grew up an only child. No one realized the impact this had on him until his mother once found him staring at the wall, his chin planted on his fists.

"What're you thinking of?" she asked.

"My children will never know what it is like to have an aunt or an uncle," he answered.

Alas, Médi never even got married, because he was killed in a traffic accident one day on his way home from school. His mother was in France, so Othman's family rushed to assist him in his calamity, as the tradition dictates. This took place in spite of the chill that had come upon his relations with his family since his marriage.

Thérèse arrived the next morning. She walked through the wide-open front door and fainted. People thought that it was due to the child's death, and she was of course struck by the death, but her fainting was caused by the sight of her house full of natives in white djellabahs and fezes, chanting and burning incense!

The shock was so great that her physician had to be called. When she regained consciousness, she remembered immediately what had happened and rushed to Médi's room. His body lay on a wooden board, wrapped up except for the face in a white cloth, exactly like a mummy. A *faqih* was leaning on the board and Othman was standing nearby. Thérèse walked up to her husband, her livid face contracting in anger. She slapped him with the right hand, then with her left. She grabbed the faqih by his djellabah hood, dragged him, and threw him out against a wall. Then, turning towards the visitors and the Qur'an reciters, she mumbled something and pointed to the front door where some people were picking the faqih up and helping him to adjust his clothes.

When the last person left, Thérèse slammed the door shut and grabbed the phone. She called first her parish priest, then the funeral home, and then her relatives and friends. Minutes later, the house was full of black European suits and hats.

The priest went to Médi's room, stripped the body of its shroud, and Thérèse dressed it with Médi's best clothes. The child was put in a smooth wooden coffin lined with green velvet, and the coffin was placed in a black hearse covered with wreaths of roses in every color. The funeral procession then made its way, first to the church where the coffin was carried in, preceded by the cross and the priest mumbling prayers in Latin, then to the Christian graveyard.

Moha and the Sea

Moha lives in the mountains, a half-day ride away from the nearest village. In spite of his seventy years, he still, thank God, goes down to the weekly market on a mule, once a month at least. He takes chickens, eggs, farm butter, and fresh and sour milk, and comes back with a store of candles and matches.

Every time the people in the village see Moha, they ask him: "When ya gonna see the sea?" Everybody in the village and its vicinity, no matter how unimportant, has seen the sea. Everybody except him. He answers that the sea is at the end of the world and he is busy. It is true that he is always plowing or harvesting or threshing or picking fruits or cutting thorns to fortify the enclosure fence, or mending his roof again.

Besides, where is he going to get the money? No ticket to Casablanca costs less than the price of a sheep, at least. Let alone expenses in the cities, where even water costs money. One needs a fortune to see the sea, and he is a mere laborer, toiling all day long, no income, no salary, unless he comes upon some buried treasure, but that does not happen anymore of course. Let them say what they like, he cannot afford to see the sea.

One morning, however, Moha had an idea. He went down to the weekly market, relied on God, and sold the mule with its pair of saddlebags, and hopped into a truck headed toward Casablanca. He sat down in the passenger's seat and took out from the hood of his djellabah a little bundle in which he had tied up the mule money. He drew out a one-hundred dirham note and handed it to the driver. Then retied the bundle neatly, put it back into the hood, and tucked the hood behind him.

Soon, the truck was swinging up and down the mountains slopes, and Moha was smiling at the images crossing his mind and saying to himself: "I'll get off at the sea. I won't set my feet anywhere but the sea. I'll see the sea and have one of those photographers take my picture there. Then I'll get into a taxi, and I'll go to that hotel that's named on the piece of paper." He pulled his hood, felt the paper under the mule money, and tucked the hood again between himself and the back of the seat. He addressed the driver: "They say that the sea is big."

"Very big!"

"Is it twice as big as the lake?"

"Twice?" echoed the driver, shaking so hard with laughter that they nearly ran off the road. "Twice?" he repeated. "No! It's millions, billions of times the surface of the lake. The sea, you see, old father, is what they call infinite waters."

"Oh my!" exclaimed Moha, taking off his djellabah. "This seat is as hard as a rock." He folded the djellabah on his knees, slid it beneath him, and sat on it, saying: "How on earth can you get used to these seats?"

The driver resumed his concentration on the winding road across his windscreen, bordered with a red velvet fringe from the middle of which dangled a cluster of artificial grapes. Moha resumed his thoughts. Suddenly, he said in a whisper: "I need to make water."

The driver stopped without pulling up. Moha hopped down. He unwound his knees. "I feel as if I had been shackled," he exclaimed. In the utter silence, all he heard was the grind of the engine. He made for the rear, turned his back to the road while the truck bumped and ground. He looked over his shoulder. The truck was leaving with his djellabah and his mule money, groaning and moaning and blowing smoke. Moha stayed in the middle of the road, swinging his arms up and down, staring at the vehicle until it faded away and he could no longer hear its hum.

Moha has not yet seen the sea, and now has decided he does not want to see it.

Glossary

Djellabah: a full, loose robe with a hood, usually of cotton or wool.

Dirham: silver Moroccan coin worth approximately a half dollar in U.S. money.

Faqih: theologian versed in the religious law of Islam.

Inshallah: an expression meaning, "If Allah wills it."

Kohl: a preparation used to darken the edges of the eyelids.

Mashrabiah: lattice-like panels used to adorn the windows in traditional housing.

Tayammun: ablution with sand, a concession for those who cannot find water or would be harmed by constant use of it.